MR. RODNEY PAUL WILLIAMS'
A Short Story Series 1

RODNEY PAUL WILLIAMS

authorHOUSE

AuthorHouse™
1663 Liberty Drive
Bloomington, IN 47403
www.authorhouse.com
Phone: 833-262-8899

Published by AuthorHouse 08/23/2023

ISBN: 979-8-8230-1331-4 (sc)
ISBN: 979-8-8230-1335-2 (e)

Library of Congress Control Number: 2023915267

Print information available on the last page.

This book is printed on acid-free paper.

CONTENTS

About the Author vii

I AIN'T FRAID OF NO GHOSTS

Chapter One 1
Chapter Two 18
Chapter Three 25
Chapter Four.. 30

5 SOUTHERN BELLES 37

PREVERT – PART 1

Chapter One 57
Chapter Two 64
Chapter Three 69
Chapter Four.. 71
Chapter Five.. 73
Chapter Six 77
Chapter Seven 79
Chapter Eight... 83

Chapter Nine 84
Chapter Ten 86
Chapter Eleven.. 89
Chapter Twelve 91

ABOUT THE AUTHOR

My history is in my books, so to all you other authors try this on for size.

I take imaginative liberty.

My mom was Venusian, a Princess. One of her parents four princesses. Oh and there was one uncle too.

My mom was there step-sister.

My Dad, a dethroned king, devoid of family, friends and fortune. I guess my mom took pity on him, so here I am.

Try that on far size.

Mr. Rodney Paul Williams

A.k.a

Rodney Paul Banks

I AIN'T FRAID OF NO GHOSTS

CHAPTER ONE

The ending came to him a moment too a minute or two minutes after he came conscious from his slumber. All he needed now was the middle to the end of the filler between that and his very good beginning. The decision, write the ending, stowe it and create the middle from there.

This is only the beginning. Broken tail reflector and deep scratch on the side. I already questioned the driver. A priest. Just keep a watchful eye on them. Claims he just left claymore mansion. Moved out. Says the place is haunted. Gave him the full intox course. He passed in all. Ghost! Come back car five. Yeah. Fifty four, out.

The corporal having had turned up his uniform jacket's collar to ward off the beginning of a second month of this year. Tahos New Mexico's frigid air turns the color back down. Entering his supervisors patrol car, the heater he left on when beginning his just ended investigation. Seated door closed and beginning to goodly warm himself, a freezing chill grips his person, yet only for a second. His inquisitiveness ends with the returning warmth.

On the day of moving into their new mansion one curious thing happened. The house changed it's color. Noticeable to the whole family moving in the entire teal wintering changed to mint. The wife and mother took a quick look. The customery blink and shake of the head from left to right caused an it must have been my imagination as the second blink revealed the real sightable. The quick change neglected.

Danner's anger shows only a smouldering of the rage disguised by concern for her little ones even before the fleeing away of her short lived in abode. But at this instant and a few more instants joined to this one her raging anger completely excepted the camoflague of true disdain and fear.

She took a few moments to pull it together and engage the cosmetic mirror. The chill in her, hairy follicles on her well developed saliva dripping from any mans mouth thick muscular thinghs and calves, yes she is hairy, along with their family on her arms and the crown of beaty adorning her oh so awesomely shaped pate stood straight up. Her head of long luxurious strands long but now stiff did not flow with the wind bursting through her opened shot gun seats door window.

They tried to harm my family was in full charge over the other reasons her mind sought revenge. Still not yet aware of her families angst of the horror presently in full command of their senses.

When the parson excepted the payment plan sealing the deal he made one stipulation. The eight car garage must be renovated to accommodate his recreation vehicle before he arrived. It was done on time.

Once in a while what happens, happens right. The police car arrived right along side of the paramedics ambulance.

The carpenter died. You say the garage doors that you are replacing were on the lawn here? Yes. And the workman was by the horses outing trimming for the garages new ceiling over there? Yes. Now if what you report is correct, then how in hell did the garage material get from here to over where his body is and slice him in half? I don't.

Midsef, the eldest sat in back of the family r.v. her hands held her ipod, her ears stopped-up by ear plugs put the contraption on the folded sofa beds arm and the shaking of her body became more turbulent as the song son of a Preacher man ended and Ray Parker Juniors; Ghost Busters followed it.

Her complexion paled and he body felt cold. She shivered. Goosebumps were delivered from within, know lieutenant. I of course asked all my men working here. None of us know. If you look around, you will not find any equipment that could have caused that to happen. No way a bunch of the guys could have thrown that four hundred pound garage door thirty yards with enough force to do that. Those very same thoughts were still occurring and running through lieutenant Joe Columbo's computer like cop mind.

Death is a weird thing. Case in point. While lying on the asphalt driveway, Morgan Freeman, member of the Carpenters Union three years tried to reminisce a night in the future. He comes home early from work. He cooks dinner, a four case government meal for his wife of nine months. Flower pettles the bed and stairway leading the way to some. Thanks Charlie Chan, his marriage is in the best of condition. She comes in the kitchen through the two car garage. She is happily surprised. Did you know that in some small circles a kiss is called a swag? She with gentileness hugs him, legs wrapped around his hips, he is standing. She slowly, sweetly swags her husband.

Not enigmatic of his reasons her mate did not take her right on that spot as her usually would do some mild depression was on sought. When seeing a set dinner table the list of what ifs ended at the thought Carol Linders better not be beating my time. A smile came along with that one. Carol Linder's was a figment of imaginations she examined every time something unexpected happened, even for the elusive washer or dryer sock.

She would taste one or two bites of her meal and that is when it would occur. A couple hours of free loving, because he had roofed her.

Fate too is a fickle thing, but in this instance he at the least got to finish his last illusion before bleeding to death from that in some manner launched discarded garage door leaning against the wall it bloodies a centimeter of his midsection dangling from the doors while brass look.

The Parson and his family of wife and nine young'uns were leaving their mansion for three days ownership in quite hurried fashion. The travelling home of six month. Rubber burned leaving traction marks some twenty yards into the parkway. Travel.

With pressing the electronic twenty feet gate barely gave way enough. The family was doing speed as though launched from a NASA launch pad. Still the closing gate left the auto's paint a scar in both driver's side doors and the right rear quarter panel. A broken red right turn signal covering would surely have an alert police traffic officer pull them over.

The conversation would go in this manner. Pulled you over for that broken tail light. Sorry officer. We were in a hurry. The security gate was closing to fast. That why the car looks keyed? Yes. License, ownership papers and insurance verification, all produced and verified an instance happened the police officer to ask a simple single question. That scratch on your side and the plastic pieces from your rear reflector still in the housing tells me this just happened what were you in such a hurry for. They driver and his passengers were then detained for a driving under the influence test. No argument was aroused. The minister had to agree to himself quietly that had he heard the reason for such a haste, had he been the traffic cop, he would conject a safety test would be in order. A tea tottler, non-smoker and no illegal narcotics user he had no problem passing the basic examinations. He passed the hand stretched out to touch his nose, the walking a straight line test and a breathilizer before being wished well and allowed on his way.

Maybe he is just insane. I got no test for that said the two striper after the family was only a few yards forward.

He gets on his squad cars radio. Car fifty four to car five. Come in Jake. Car five here. Go ahead fifty four here. Jake there's an orange family trailer.

There is the understanding many funerals umbrella are in use. Goes to movite most horrific unsurreal deaths occur on bright starlit nights as they do on beautiful sunny days. How is the weather were you are?

The chill told the r.v. driving preacher to drive the vehicle at full speed. He did so. Most drivers would have eased off the gas pedal when on a downhill droving highway. Not what happened. The result was the forty five foot dromonal Reo pulled trailer driver eyes met the preacher's.

The pieces of both vehicles....

The cold is intense. Renard the only boy child the preacher and his wife would ever parent in his sleep while dreaming of one of his future employment scenarios, on television the news reporter Smailliw luap was reporting on the tenth child to disappear this month was given a mental message from his agent, Renard "the preachers son" before I make you a superstar us, you and I make your not suffer the feeling of being beneath you. After all she is your mom. Naturally she will be proud of you anyway, but what if we make he famous, a communications superstar who gets the idea to help you with your career. Then we bring you up. Just below her status mind you.

Both Renard and he felt good with that. Both believing, maichistae, the reporter's mother received the mental communicate.

This type of career seemed to fulfill his awareness in his dream. One thing it had actually done was release. The fear from the haunted house he and his family are now fleeling.

Awakened fully aware of his surroundings, the cold showed him his real future the large vehicles collided one tenth of one second later.

On the same day as the pastor, his wife and children perished the short time of agony, of pain of crushed bones of pierchings and gasoline mingles diesel fuel blazing fire, the neighbor living next door to the tractor trailer driver drying in the same manner, only with her the diesel fuel mingled with the rv's gasoline her husband was being visited by Samuel the legal Eagle, Wilson.

Joe Hopscotch listened intently to his neighbor. And why should he not. Wilson had only yesterday won a verdict getting his client found not guilty for a murder where there were witnesses and camera videos showing his client in the act of taking the lives of three dark brown skinned women. The trial had been televised all over the planet.

That was not his first publicized win in such a manner. Lips and Brain, the legal equivalent to the most posh of magazine at the end of the case still in the courtroom gave Wilson his monogramed request letter to allow the magazine to award him lawyer of the year. It paid Wilson ten million dollars too.

Jolene Jobeth Hopscotch had to things done for her own behalf when summoned to the sitting room by her brother Abet.

J.J. Dad and Mister Wilson are in the chat room. Dad says for you to come in there immediately. He sounds solemn. Mister Wilson looks businesslike. What you did you can tell us later. Sounds important. Jolene turned off her Dell computer, she got from her wicker chair a mate to her desk. As she left her room Abet softly let a hand to her left shoulder. Be careful sis. Dad also told me to make sure none of us except you come in there until he gives us the nod. Abet knew his younger sister hung out with a crowd to be leery of. He went into his other two siblings bed room. Knock first Dipstick! Mildly shouting warned his next to youngest sister Jillette.

Jentile the youngest girl was at her desk studying where she might get the best exposure to boys her age that sold Skelcher light-up tennis foot wear.

The conversation took hours. Jousting back and fourth until the lawyer had completely explained, re-explained and again explained every aspect of the laws the Hopscotch child would have to face.

Finally the father and his daughter clearly knew avenue of the charges the common wealth would use to punish Joe Lene. The lawyer advice seemed best and mister Hopscotch decradled the land line, an old Victorian Cradle modle. He dialed nine one.

The police operator identified herself. Inquired what the emergency was and since being in that department for were a decade lended no shook in the caller turning his daughter in, she being one of students who attacked the old transient on the public subway train. The students face were covered due to COVID-19 public transit regulations. Operator six four nine seven dispatched the message over the radio to all patrol cars in the callers identified area.

Three and a half hours earlier a meeting began that ended in three and a half hours commenced.

You're going to need to know how to handle this. Did you see the news last night about the four school kids? You mean the one on the Uptown N train? The one the old hobo got attacked? Yes. That one. Man Jolene has a jacket exactly like one of the kids. Her shoe that the rider was beaten with. I've seen on your daughter a few times. Hell man she passes right in front of me everyday on her way to school. She's my next door neighbor. You're her father. Why didn't you notice it was your own daughter with those other thugs? Sooner or later, most likely sooner someone's going to not only recognize her as I did, but they're going to phone up the police. Get ahead of them. I'll help you. If you don't. Then I won't.

Joe Hopscotch viewed his son A out on the lawn. He tapped on the closed screen sliding door. His son's attention captured. Go get me Jolene, send her here immediately. Then you and your sister- do not bother us- unless it is serious.

Abet heads towards the stairs, yellow and green marbling on both sides of a thick Berricelli carpet. The staircase is six feet wide and the ornate pomegranate and bell filigreed silver inlaid baluster supports the twenty one foot long slightly curved alabaster coping.

J.J to her being verbally scolded, lectured and tutored. Those are the same stairs that lead.

The same stairway that would lead to her eventual freedom. Freedom from her participation from the heinious and violent crimes she did commit.

While Jolene listened intently the plan was laid out without a single insufficiency.

Neither she nor her co-harts faces were seen. She had assumed if none of her villians opened their mouth than no one would be able to catch them. She had too seen the video of their attacking the homeless guy on the news. Things appeared to her inexperienced self-cool.

What her now legal representative clearly opened her mind to was that all of the people the police would be searching for were school students getting or the train after school left out. Add to that her teachers would not only know one hundred percent what she wore to and from school that day but it is fairly believable some of her teachers would know who her girlfriends in school are. So would the goody-two-shoes classmates who saw them together every day. Closing out any discrepency that may have entered Jolene's mind Sam Wilson also knew her tight girlfriends and without doubt the four of the culprit girls names rolled of his tongue. She knew none of their faces were shown on the news reel. Her dad's condemning stare sealed it.

The lawyers cell phone rang. It was Frank Engel the former defendant of Wilson's second miracle non guilty verdict. The miracle in that case was Engel had no alibi. Engel had threatened the rapist of Danial O' Learhy, a nine year old curly red headed, fair skinned boy, Cameras had Engel in the area at the time of the killing. When all of that had surfaced, Engel gave a verbal confession and signed the written one on the dot-dot line. Denial is Frank's godson.

Engel's words came over the receiver. Good to hear from you man. Your last one hundred eighty eight thousand has just been deposited. I can never tell you how much I love you man. Laura is waiting. She says hey. The phone clicked.

The trio seaked in comfortable nine inch thick fast filled pillow seat cusions but only the lawyer felt at being in a modicum of ease. Jolene tense and ill at ease, gathered she was beated about the subway train incident yet a glimmer of hope.

Her father pissed off at his the thought of owning her choked in his brain. It did not expel.

Jolene's glimmer died. If you open your mouth even once until we tell you to I will fricassee your behind came from the man forcing himself to remember this meeting was to save his daughter, daughter came through that time and he did take it in that this was more than an attempt to reclaim his flesh and blood, from an arrest conviction, incarceration, possible lesbianism and a dead end future.

His face give no clue to the heat building up in him. He had by forced effort of his own taken notice of the young girls crotch as she first seated herself. Her yellow thong not even daring to try to keep court a fully hairy spread. She did not groom with a razor there. Both sides and the bottom of her underware had poured her vaginal crown outwards. Her legs folded under her now the picture remained. He went on with his legal barrage necessary to twart justice.

The police arrived at the front gate.

Officers Madello O'Brien and Blonten Zisk both took notice of a cell phone on the inside of table by the sitting room entrance. The two walked into the room at the behest of the man of the house. The lawyer and his client Jolene sat in silence.

On the stairway leading to the bedroom are the other three offspring. As in his training officer Zisk glances the blind spots from the front door until he has entered the sitting room. He did take full notice of the children. During the briefing given them he almost completely forgot about them. Neither the father nor the two city cops even gave a seconds thought to the cell phone on the table. The phone still recording every word.

So much is going on downstairs it is all but impossible having attention on the three young one upstairs. The two older Abet and Dexeilia Abigai sit in that joining are a where the upper hallway meets the crowning step, gathering difficulty. Dexeillia asks her older brother what is the name of the area where they sat. What area? She explained. The place where the hallway meets the top tied running her finger on the marble tied and the panels, touching again with her finger both sides of the marble panels and finally with her pointer finger the carpeted riser step.

His genius mind and teaching part click in. He decides not to pull one over on her. Not this time. Best to stay serious with the goings on down stairs. A short answer, the American languages has none. Please hold on to anything else until we know what is the conclusion pointing downstairs.

The youngest has now joined them. She informs them Buster's kidnapped. Mrs. Millen on the news just reported the story. Proud of using the phrase just reported rather than just said. Who stole him wants ten million dollars or before thanksgiving or they are going to eat him. The kidnapped Buster's is the name of the Thanksgiving bird reprieved via presidential pardon. It had been on its way to Disney world to preside over the holiday's parade.

Abet paid almost no attention to his turkey caring sister. Then the thought could CIA security have just been tested? And failed.

Officers sit down this is going to take a bit of explaining came his father's voice from the family meeting room.

Picturing the news report, I hereby pardon you Buster's you are now free from being thanksgiving day's main course. The picture lingered as he had viewed the report on his bedroom one hundred inch projected on the ceiling. Though crossed his mind, have all pardon turkeys over the years been white.

As young as he was he could not expel the exam in his head. If black lives matters came from an anti racist view point then why did we, most Americans being we celebrate this most racist of occasions.

Country western music could not even have saved the original inhabitants, so the joke goes.

His minds sharpness was attacked so numerous of times with those last few thoughts. Good thing I am recording the conversation downstairs.

Jolene had missed nothing. She was ripped up inside. Hold back the tears. Do not hold my niagra. Her visage on her face too was adorned. Wicked confliction.

Sorrow depressed her and her face hid the rest of her tears in her brothers pajama shirt pocket beginning the wetness. Seconds ago one of droplets left her right eye ball abandoning the others. The tear had for a short time plenty of companions first the lower eyelid it swelled up behind rolled over the edge. It met a few short curvy eyelashes, the out part of that eyelid rolling down it to the upper part of the skin on a high cheek bone. The moist droplet bred by sadness, worry and fear might have traveled the full of her jaw but for her chin resting on her clavicle. All those parts kept the salt water company until it took the lonely fall from her cheek highlighted by the hallways two fluorescent lights, one in yellow the other in pale pink. Their mother's design for when she was way for days up to a week doing her job.

The loneliness desisted on the ninety five percent cotton, five percent polyester night gown in dinosaur picturesque boutique. Just above her knee recognized the moisture after the materials saturation. Her face sank to Abet's chest for comfort from the words of the talkative adults below on the first floor of house, her home. The flood came quietly muffled by her siblings garment.

For the first time since alighting and ease dropping she did not hear the voices.

Abet and petite FN however heard it. FN's slight head jerk aligned with her quizzical look on her face alerted her big brother that at some time in the near future he may have to explain the lawyers articulation as her father went to answer the front doors chiming. Tell no one, said quietly but with a guiding forcefulness married to it, except the judge while you are on trial that you are not sorry for what you did, but you are aware that you should be for doing someone wrong and that you are working on becoming a better female so that you will recognize that you are sorry. I guarantee you no prison time. After the police came in from entering the front door with there father Jolene did exactly as the three of them had her rehearse. She never said a word and she could have won an Emmy with the I am so so sorry face. Her eyes even reddened and watered. Which may have been realization and regret. Police on some occasions rub people in such a manner.

Comforting can be done the same as getting comforted with no awareness on ones body movements. Somehow that sounds incorrect if as reported by thousands of neurological scientists conclusion the brain controls the body's movement.

Abet's wet loosely buttoned pajama bottoms cratch now has his sobbling tearful sister's full frontal face weeping with slight spasms in direct contant. Gravity doing its part. Jolene remains crumpled Abet's left arm on her shoulder and back. FN's little face and her low sprine both arms crabling a hip, not yet able to circumference.

Downstairs the performance, briefed as she was was of epic proportion.

The script, her briefing given to her by the award winning attorney deserved an Oscar for best writer of a daytime drama. He put it together before the sun went down. He only delayed until Jolene's dad came in from work. Even the part where he told Jolene of the speech for the judge only when her father went to the door to let in the local authorities.

Fluffer Nutter looked so innocently beautiful carry to find who it was her sister victimized and when she got bigger should she beat the girl up too.

Sam Wilson had previously found the D.A.'s telephone number assigned to the violent attackers should their names evolve in order for their prosecution. The two, Silson and Al Flemming the D.A. agreed to meet at the precinct to meet the surrenderee and her attorney, being as how his secretary was somehow informed by him to alert the news crews. All the stations agreed. I'll have a camera crew there in a few shakes. The arrest at the precinct was agreed to be ten minutes later than necessary. The camera crews. The D.A.'s publicity coverage. And Sam Wilson superstar lawyer. Promotion gleamed in the emerald spectators of Flemming.

Jolene had been so preoccupied with contain and maintaining legal directions she had neglected to keep track of time, although earlier in day after returning home from school she remember to detract but at that time decided to delay the pads assertion blocking her soon to flowing vagina's crimson tide.

It did happen in the patrol car. She alerted officer Rechiel, the driver. He in turned radioed the station, through her he attained her lawyers phone number. The cause was approved by the station's supervisor. The corporal phoned Sam Wilson, her attorney and given the proper instructions, he stopped by Rite-Aid.

When the came came through Sam Wilson had just a second or to before heard the sweetness of Sharon Davis. His Brain betrayed present day reality. The sweetness went from hears to his nostrils. He wafted his mind in her frankencense. Sharon Davis the nineteen year old ten thousand dollar a right prostitute. The in crowd knows. She will mayor next election.

Sex is always one of his highest adjudicators. However his clients are always without restriction save for his own being and God above, above him, paramount.

He tapped the security guard on the left uniformed hip. Keep your eyes on me the University Corporation guard was told. The culprit had not came near the Rite – Aid exit yet. Waiting in line with the box of comfort inside maxi pads, he loudly sneezed and asserted his way into cashier's guards and three others attention. When the candy thief tried to exit the lawyer caught the security guards eye and with outwardly deliberateness nodded his his forehead towards the thief.

The fight was short.

Before leaving Wilson turned from the checkout counter retrieve Cadbury Caramellos. The candy bars cost alone he knew would be over three dollars along with the pads eight dollars and some change came back from his Jackson.

He changed his thought from using his T.D. Bank debit card. He did not relish the box of feminine pads on his statement. He is a bachelor and he has no children.

The event of the caught and handcuffed candy thief behind him he left the drug store.

As though the sound of a Dick Wolf created television shows, Law and Order Special Victims unit theme music caresses his mind, it appears most of the people in the city realizes it's entertainment value.

As sharp and as intelligent a lawyer should maybe comprehend, the theme music is from a series dealing with the catching and convictions of rapist attached to justice for the victims unwanted attachments. Now with the reporting and apprehension of a confections purloiner.

His country western music fettish takes a hold of his radio. Not in Boise. Nor even in Idoho. Still his cars adhere to KISSIN is in both Boise and Idaho. Ahhhh! Rodeo. Ahhh! It's the country studio Crew Jammin on Garth Brooks. He commencerates the song flattening the ahhs. Rodeo, Garth Brooks.

He does not complete his listening to his habitual glee. He has arrived. The thunder Rolls but for Jolene he squelches his delectable.

Without having to gather his breath, he unlocks the driver's side door with verbal command driver's side front door unlock.

Scantily clad see through side on bouses and slacks she guides the female prevent through the prisoner's entrance door on the side of the building.

Leaving the side parking lot Wilson traversed the two flights of steps.

Each had no more nor no less than four stoney entrenched hard cement steps.

The fragrance of orchard like, lily and lilac floral fragrance hit him immediately as his first leg entered the thirty seventh precinct's entrance way. His approval was commanded. The opulence of the aromatic air aside I am Mister Sam Wilson attorney. I am here to represent Miss Jolene Hopscotch hoping the Miss rather than Ms. did not catch the train that rolls right over their bridge. Bridge an allonym for head, reminding the officers Jolene is still a young child. No matter the charge. Future planning? His thought forced a denial of the present sometimes influenced the future. He was led to the precinct supervisor.

The corporal's visage. Sloppy. Shoes unshined. No neck tie. Holster has seen for better days. Still, perhaps a future Serpico. The seventeen ribbons decorating his uniform blouse was the only clue. Then came clincher. Those blue-white eye balls green crystalline eyes with a few flecks of Caucasian brindling. They actual sparkled. A longer momentary settling of light in them and they glistened. Even the eye-ball blue. This man is sharp.

Give me a moment said the corporal. I try to always be ready and at my best. But I going for my p.h.d. and my dumb self chose a thesis that is almost impossible to document, evidence. Wilson already having two phd's his interest somewhat piqued, what is it? Your thesis I mean. The supervisor's reply comes. I chose this one, in the venerable words of former president John Fitzgerald, Kennedy, not because it's easy, but because it's hard.

I titled it are all newborn girls vagina's at thee integument the same shape or does having penile penetration cause a diversities along the way?

The corporal elaborated, getting around on the internet, scheeech. The FBI's.

Very little if at any time in the past has Sam Wilson been truly stymied. He thought. Stumped to stage of embarrassment until his calling brought him back. There it was, Jolene, Jolene. The words that finally came out of his mouth, whoo, good luck with that.

I am not sleepy. F.N. was getting on a huge anry. Determined to stay diligent until her family was all home and waiting for mommy to come home from work.

Her devotion even for such a young one untainted by let downs augments and disappointments of others. Reward surely must wait for her in the near future and the distant one the same.

Three minutes later her first reward arrived. It arrived on the tide of time and the softness and comfort in the middle of stuffed couch so lenient the bossoms of Dolly Parton would take a distant second, such could only lead to quiet, soft breathing, slumber with a silent sigh straight into dreamland. The soon to be oncoming dream would become one of her most warm hearted favorites. This one she saved her presidents life along the whole CIA and their wives and children.

She came only with the recipe and made the bomb equivalent to the West Buster, Spain's newest bomb to scare the USA into buying toys broke real, really easy and had no refunds and no exchange.

Her bomb, boys "R" Yucky, was made of dish washer rinse water, the extra large carogated tube of cleanser, a hidable detonator and the left eye of Abet's mosest favorite G.I. gorilla doll. Even if Abet used to argue with her the toy is not a doll fluffer Mutter. It is an action figure.

Somewhere in her dream in a mist, a cloud making it invisible to dis-earn was a figure unable to view by any except FU was a slyly smiling almost seeable face, seeable only to FN mouthing quietly, understandable to her only, an action figure with only one eye. And her own mind. I bet you won't only leave me one elegant with yellow icinged drum on his back next county Fair day.

Hmmm, as she self assuredly rolled from her side to full out prone position on flat lying frontal body. Except for that one left leg. Every time she slept so smugly that left knee was always bent in a hundred an ten degree angle. Knee touching her left almost fisted a little world saving hand. One and only one fingernail painted. Mom wasn't home. Only mommy paints all my nails. Just little Daddy only let her point his nales. When she is awake and not dreaming of course.

An aspect of reality had with notice invaded dreamland asserting no warning, no awareness what-so-ever of in pending doom a change in life, one unwanted, one feared and although it first appeared in her sleep, the quiet bell soon of awakening creepily, silently extols and evlogizes, soon, soon soon.

As was their custom when spending a week or so with the grands the little ones both boys bestrum three and the eldes Benedict almost five never knocked on a closed door. The huge double master bedroom was also included in their youthful disdain of all privacy. Super here strength a Herculeen feet to Steve Reeves the double obstruction.

When the doors opened grandpa sat at the bed's end shirtless Grandma aware of her heirs, heirs procliuities never missed a strake and truth be told only minimally did her neck and head rhythm decrease their proclivity at opening any door unannounced having been well gotten used. The grandes visited much as mom a huge movie director and dad usually mom's executive producer and off times special Guest Star took great precautions with their offspring in today's unnatural desires for young children. Thus the grandparents. The least expensive best child caretakers on this here Earth.

The air coded comforter fully camoflagued grandma on the Louis Vuitton pillows cradling her two naked knees. Grandma's dishabille on the carpet. Her nudite still opaqued.

The seventy two year old woman defif the effigy of time. There was only one female whose crowing glory match the figure now servicing mate of fifty one years. She was now off directing Hollywoods latest blockbuster soon to be.

She and four others in her field have the strangling Hollywood now gasping for air rather than as it had been, unconscious from the former land grabbing Japanese which had the city all but called dead and autopsied. Perhaps some payback for the internment of World War 2.

Just think. Somewhere someones man, wife daughter someones loved one anyway ain't comin home tonight. Go on home. Kiss peg and Bob. They might not know but you do. So be damn glad for them that you can go home, and a family to go home to.

Men do often look in one another's eyes. This is one of those times when an I'll see you tomorrow can shut down a conversation. While in his minds forefront his commander also thinks but keeps his thoughts checked.

As his workmate drives off. Away. Home. Sure going home to Peg is a good thing. Why do the two of you taint it with a third. Your ass is spreading. And your lips show just how wide that dick is you and Peg have been sucking. What happened to the good de days when America was a one nation under Gods country. He now departs home to house with a college grand and the grads son and daughter (he smiles genuinely) and his daughter-in-law about to cash in the multi mil lottery. Yeah! He smiles. Didactically. The curse of a caring human being stifled a true jubilation. For no apparent reason his brain is haunted by the television episode. Put a sardine in the postal slot and drop it on the saucer for my... he dumps everything else and there is vision of his anguish destroyer. A two story Greek revival and seven bedrooms. Not attempting to solve the puzzle, he satisfies his savage breast. Somewhere in there. There is home. Protest is home, waiting is dinner. Longing is protest. If you would seek him now, forget about it, you probably with global tensions, political unrest and racial violent outbreaks have more enemy's than you care to have. Leave him with her and the children, you may have a friend.

Mark Tuttle was about to head on back to his room. He hissed his finger and lightly pressed it against Aganess's forehead. Without having to look she gave her good feeling sense of approval.

Aganess the head nurse of Pennsville Rothman and Elaine Rothman Hospital had been on duty those nineteen some odd years ago when Mark's mom puttered Mark on out of there. Seven pounds exact. She has loved and help raise that boy eversince. Hey Mark! She calls as he waits for the up elevator. Bite me!! She finishes. For now. She will give her sometime the detail tomorrow.

The elevator indicator lights up. Up. He sends as acknowledging pointer finger and a sideways glance.

Aganess has a youthful way of giving an invite to eat. Aganess Bledsce's plates at the county have had to increase in number of plates for the last fifteen county fairs.

Even old Mrs. Grossenbet had to give way to Aganess's cooking. It had been that way every since Mercedi, Aganess's mother and Mrs. Grossenbet's closest ally since grade school. Secretly all the other women loved Aganess though few would admit why. On county fair weekend no matter how they and your man were getting along, should one wait he soon would be found at Aganess's table.

The couple had purchased the doorbell at Walmart's Department Store before the first of the four children were born. It was advertised in the store. The Hopscotch did know it was a true item. A television show used the idea of it as a comedic foil.

He was so elated he had it. She was demurely pleased her hardworking, loving husband had a new and useful long lasting toy. She enjoyed it best on let's pretend night. He stayed in form. Feigning to have forgotten his front door key, usually it was still on the ring with those of the Volvo.

He would savor pushing the button. While on the inside before the children she gave herself leave way to question, who could that be when hearing the someone's at the door called out by the mechanical device.

All these years later she still helped keep her mind young and active. She never allowed her mind to allow the answer to the question whom it could be in her house telling her someones at the door.

Over the years she silently congratulated herself for her earnest all out commitment of denying the door's voice as a mechanical device even when she realized one after the other of children learned vocalization.

Her presence is always anticipated when she was on the road. He presence is missing now- heavily.

Jolene showered, said her prayers and looked in on her siblings, then went to bed.

Okay man. Your children are all in tight, what do want. Why did you ask me to wait?

I watched the news while you represented Jolene at the precinct. Just as said the reporters put you on. My family had two bulletins on the show. Jolene's and Evelyn's. Evelyn's come the lawyer's questioning response to Jo Hopscotch Evelyn's gone. Her semi crashed head on into a family camper. She's gone.

The detectives called me first, before the broadcast hit the sorene. She is dead Jo Hopscotch heart was in his eyes. There, waiting to be alone was Niagra Falls.

Dexeilia Abigail is the middle daughter. Until the call came she had fallen asleep. Someone at the door. Dexeilia drowsily shook he head. She came to the top staircase and made a start downwards. She saw her father finger Sam Wilson into silence. Being discovered barely, slightly took a glance at her, still, she waited.

The Chief of Unsolved Cases Division, Two star, General Cold, Case sat at home his legs crossed just above the thin as tooth pick sized ankels and on the Ashati Stool hassack sized lighted the flat of his palm on the enormous volumned buttocks of Linda Melicia Benedict Cold, his, you can use another cold one smiling spouse.

CHAPTER TWO

The thirteen military corpses arrived at La Bonia Naval Base on a bright hot clear sky sunnt day. They had all been murdered serving their country. They had been assigned to the very important and world publicized force guarding the retreat of American serviceman's support system. Thousands of men women and children being returned home safely guarded after their country lost the war against Afghanistan.

All was going well.

The public had been told by their government the all thousands of their citizens could be evacuated in the time agreed to by both governments winners and losers. The public was lied to by the losers.

The lie because apparent when the end date of the withdrawal neared and the masses left on the foreign land were too numerous to get out by the agreed date.

Dignity should have been invoked while requesting of the Afghanees more time. It was clear to all peoples both involved and not more time would be needed. Surely respectful talk would have allowed two or three more days.

What the victorious government got was, however an unnecessarily rash insult. The losers of the war viciously stated – we will take, underline noticeably emphasize the word "take" more time to get our people out if we need it logistics sis already prove more time was needed. The threat was a nasty thing to vocalize by the leader of the country that lost the twenty year long war.

Two days later three bombs exploded in the areas were the departees were housed and an area the departees were disembarkment.

The area of disembarkment took the lives of the thirteen unnecessarily murdered military men were eleven US Marines, one US. Army and one US. Navy men including Ssgt Nicole Cole the only female.

Somewhere in the United States of America a small quiet voice rang out loudly why can a President get away with their murder. The voice with a paunty of social exposure was aware that in that country when you verbalize something and people die because of your verbalization you must be charged legally for their deaths.

The ghosts of one female, twelve male military men should along with the voices of the number of other who died in the bombings needed do haunt their own families and other people of the world. Shriek Justice.

Til this date the President of the United States of America may not only simply appear to rest easy on the matter while he looks every day as though that matter does not exist.

The other real question and perhaps it is a much more vast question to his neglecting the Afghanistan one is, does he believe hiding behind the now opposing Russia militaries the borders of Ukraine to hind behind?

The name coming up is a fake one only because the real name being used could cause the womans husband higher authority than this author cares to do.

Mrs. Josh White's wife Corsette Missle White held the meeting of the most powerful wives of the most powerful wives of the Arian Race, the Ku Klux Klan and the next three most powerful white supremist organizations.

That small voice came into her ear via mental telepathy. She wanted to answer it, the President is Democrat. All their groups were formed from the Democratic Party.

Her heart poured for justice. She wanted him impeached. That is not what the meeting was held over. The meeting specifically was on the subject that should the women proceed the impeachment most definitely would occur. The president would serve the rest of his life behind the doors of a most secure prison fill will luxuries. And the Vice President becoming president as is the law would need to be removed before the impeachment.

The woman are the most powerful women in the USA. The women are white. The women detest blacks and will not suffer the insult of a nigger woman sitting in that office rolling over them. One day God forbid all of them held tightly to that may happen but never as long as there was a white breathe in their lungs would nigger woman be the first in that White House. Never a damn care came to being that her tree hanging (private intended here) husband is white. Another insult to white purity.

The Red Hat Society sponsored there new member awakening luncheon at two post meridian in the second most stylishly elegant Platinum Slipper's crystal Room. Normally the congregation on this date every two years graced the Diamond Broach Glom. The Hotel rearranged the groups setting. The Red Hat society as estinguished as they are were bumped by Mrs. Theoleta Lee Thompson. The states most prestigious attorney while representing the friends of one Mrs. Corsette Missile White's Belles.

The Red Hat Society was sent the arrangement of one hundred dozen long stem red roses compliments of the Belles Women's Auxillery's Secretary Mrs. Joe Ann Bobby Atty. At law. Of the world reknown Bobby, Bobby and Sharpe's Law Firm.

The accompanying card read- you shall with a delightful heart and attitude, please forgive this large as life intrusion. You'll thank us later.

One day ago.

I want that lounge. Your Red Hat Society group will just have to wait. Put them in the Platinum Slipper. It is close to size and elegance.

Morten Sal agreed to the demand. He would give the lounge to her on a whim considering her status. He only delayed in order to find out if she wanted that group not to be allowed in the building. Since the Platinum was suggested by her as a replacement, then the RHS could still book his hotel. He was not aware of powerful influences of one of the Societies executive staff has.

One day farther backwards.

The secretary only know the date, place, time and the names of the invitees. The messages mentioned frivolous things. Unassuming things. Things not one would give a second glance. The invitees accepted with each c.s.u.p. only one said a single word, neat. All called their private pilots. One twelve passenger lear, two eight passenger helos and the last a four seat Coreolari twin engine, brand new never before in the air.

The four women arrived immaculately attired. Sofia Vargara sunglasses and a Gal Gadot wide brim. Each of the ladies also left their personal body guards behind without any statement verbal or otherwise, except she left them as the air ships door was closed.

The arrivals were similar. From the private airstrips three of the four took roadsters. Neither took the scenic route. One arrival landed directly a top the resort hotel. The VIP elevator allowed her to exit by the private swimming pool. The crystalline water reflected her a perfect still life of her image. The water had yet to be disturbed today. She more than glanced herself. In truth the hardness she had been on her reflection was exceedingly noncompliant. She for seventy years in age was absolutely pick-up up in any bar gorgeous.

The five together comprised power no government dared say no, by the meetings end their business would be complete and the process on its pertinacious.

First order of business. The trip to Bangladesh would be in two months. Ten orphanages would be visited. Gifts would be hand delivered to each child in each orphanage.

A luncheon would be held in the early day at one of children's gift ceremonies. By the middle of the trip back home word would be given to the world that all the people who ate at the meal had died of a delayed action type acid poison. Word would be let out to the poess that the Bangladesh government feared for the first lady of the United States as no contact could be made with her plane home to the US. That plan was voted down by the Belles four to one. The plan adopted was the her forced kidnapping on the way to speak at a women's auxillery circus of the US's one hundred richest women to stop abortions by better decisions on getting pregnate. After all with today's tech no woman could be impregnated against her will. Then the first lady would be placed into todays version of the underground rail read.

Moved constantly twenty four hours a day to a minimum of ten places per day. Beaten, raped and humiliated at each one them going from one side of the U.S, to the other, from one province in Canada to another and from one country in South America to Another non-stop. Then and only then with its success insured would the President be impeached.

The whole of the discussions was done in the unique code only the very tiptop of the Belles organization knew:

The women slick as a whistle each used different coded conversation. Each used a yes and no vote the sounded as peachy as mom's apple pie.

The present.

The Belles decided to take in the town for an hour on so to pick-up a few souvenirs. Metha Elfman was the deciding vote that chose Supreme Court Justice. Alex Guiness an un notable man whose legal wisdom and constitutional knowledge was second to none.

Elfman and Corsette White partnered up going to Leggo's Pescaderia to nosh on sushi and gumbo.

In the middle of lunch, Metha excused herself from the conversation of why after being married for decades men prefer their wives to wear thong panties backwards.

I gave my granddaughter my word I would call her to introduce her to you. Do you mind corsi? The two women were mutually admired by the others children and grandchildren and had been close companions for over thirty years. Therefore the familiarity in the first name calling. Of course I don't.

The never was any stumbling in conversation between these two excellent vocalist one with a doctorate from Yale. The others doctorate at Julliard.

Jenna's voice came gleefully full of excitement.

Gramma an angelic shout. Bendi, grands on the phone. Bendexterous, Jenna's older brother was on his third hour of Obo practice.

None but the power couple one equipped a set of chopsticks filigree carved and green jade inlaid finger indentations for easy manipulation knew the vote was just now cast. The president is now on his was to disagree and to prison.

Glendettenia Baxter Bendix, the one of the five who took out alone stopped by the Post office in the middle of the towns business district and sent her package guaranteed over night delivery to her husband Thedix. Thedix was at home for the next nine days. A needy vacation from heading his office overseas in Botswanna. Lieutenant General Thedix Roosevelt Bendix took a short ten days before his son retirement from the USA Air Force. He was up for AF Chief of Staff in four months also. He wanted to discuss it with his wife as four years ago he promised her he would retire this year.

Her trip took her to Lennix's Lingerie and commodities.

The package was from Lennix's. A suit for him. To be one hundred percent precise a pair of pajamas with short sleeves and short sleeves and short shorts. She was sure her husband would get the message. The suit was made of gummy candy. Glendettenia is a diabetic.

Her skills sets are organization. When the Bells needed what would take months or years of debate with men, a simple phone call from Glendettenia removed obstacles. No foreign governments black opts ever told her no. She received her post from her mother as did she receive her now deceased mother's clout. It was never said but JFK may still be alive today if her husband had not been a senior official of the Ku Klan and her mother had but shook rather than nod her head. Now it is rigueur for the death of any major player, physically, socially and or politically to address her in her mothers stead. A righteous pre-eminent leader get on her bad side and uneasy lies the head that wears the crown is a phrase you could not use. She is quick, thorough and unless she chose so, which she never has, you are done before you know. Race horses have better sight than any of her tagged ones. Her face angelic. Her hair dos always admirable. Her figure soft, supple, hour glasses, smooth, as white as writing paper, smooth, as white as writing paper, her teeth her own and gleaming while perfectly shaped, her eyes never saw more clear one brown and one violet. She needed no cosmetic make up.

She extracted a small piece of a Ritz Buttery saltine cracker and leisurely with the slightest of a half smile on the right side of her lips made thicker with time spent attending her mate tossed the remainder of it to the female pigeon strutting the sidewalk before entering the hotel.

I have you misses in sight sir. She has every look of independence and is enjoying her jambalaya and Pabst Blue Ribbon. Other than ditching her security everything is fine. O.K. than. Keep an eye on my wife from a short distance. As long as she doesn't need assistance, give her her own control of her rein. But if for one instant you see any way harm may come to her. You can bet on sir. Sweet mama's in charge. The Office of Special Investigation, Colonel in no way wished this detail, but the Major General was his personal commander. Other than the Joint Chiefs and the President he took his orders from no other with such a personal gusto Sweet Mama, as he affectionately termer his job would not been in the shower without his eyes on her. His body guard mission had turned from seek and find and he would be there should his personal specialty be called up. For a short distance. The hotel afforded no clean opportunity to get within personal arms length of her in any way. Not guest, not employee. Besides learned is the places head of security. Learner never could be compromised by the dark side. Learner had turned in his own older brother to the CIA believing his sibling a terrorist. Learner's family tie there kept him from guarding the Ellsworth Fenderton, the royal families highest ranking Earl of Bestonia. He rested easily, but his even in r.e.m sleep, awareness never slept.

During the one day stay the five females spent the of seventeen minutes in the v.i.p. hall letted to them. None save themselves know what transipations in that gamoured ehoing chamber and when they no longer had a course to manifest their whims only the seating moved from the formal set-up array did prove vacancy had been denied.

The chefs on brunch and supper both gave to the realization those five woman ate as much as any fifteen others I have ever prepared for. The shock was most of the food remained in thick healthy white skinned women that seemed never to been on the sands during summer.

There dry cleaners work would be a time of paid leisure.

The five showed themselves by the elevator upon departure. One would ascend to the roof and the private helicopter pad.

Her mate during the outing where the group separated left a one hundred dollar tip for the bell boy who had fetched the moped she mode on around town. Jeb Clampet Junior. A gleaming report she gave to him.

The Belles depart. Each in separate direction. One south one west, one east, one up and one north.

Mary the only one having had the idea of how to get rid of the president and not venture its expression again mulled it over. Cause her lover to invade the Ukraine and when that loud mouth to be put out of office threatens Russia execute a precise cut by drone. One single solitary surgical strike. The families of wronged American soldiers avenger.

Mary Jones got into her now slightly vintage nineteen ninety Excalibur, dropped the hood, put in her blue tooth ear set and voiced to her on board radio June Carter and pulled out.

In her garage at home sat parked her autos big brother, The Mercedez Benz Sak nineteen thirty two model.

CHAPTER THREE

LUCY I'M HOME

Colonel William Hurt Mensch is a Hebrew Rabbi. Colonel William Hurt Mensch stands absolutely still erect legs apart, fists balled up one on either hip. His eyes though for the last ten minutes have not waved in position, they have not even blinked while cast into the image of mirror above the wash room sink in the bathroom he alone has the authority to enter, to occupy, to make use of. And why not? This is his kingdom. His domain. He alone rules here. His will is granitized. His word is bond. He commands, it is done. This fortress is speckled with insanity. It is on any given day and on any given darkness period non-paralleled by its violence. It is the state penitentiary for the unreformable elements of those caught, found guilty in a court of law and sentence to die here in this place. Not one resident has less than the sentence of life times ten. This is Dallas State Penitentiary for the unreformable. This is his realm and his alone.

Once before in his life had he questioned his decisions. Now he finds himself questioning this one. That is the rationale for the mirrored images indefatigable stillness.

Betty Brokaw sat at her desk outside the office of Warden Mensch. She has had that desk as her own for three years. Ms. Brokaw is a certifies one hundred ninety one i.q.d. genius. She has earned he second degree in both karate and Akido. Her master's degree is simply a test away from graduation. She is a cinch to doctorate it Penal and corrections Psychology. She is devotedly Catholic.

She is in this institution to keep close communication with flip "killer" Wilson her husband of sixteen years and stepfather of her three daughter Emma, Gail and Dexti. The warden has granted her a three hour weekly conjugal visit. He is doing life times thirty. Since Betty's applying for the position he has been a model prisoner and kept his block in fairly good standings. A good deal made by Mensch.

Mensch step from the lavoratory and into his office attached through his door, his door being the side connected to his office. Exited but leaving open the side of the door on Ms. Brokaw's territory. Her having no others in her office as she sat at her desk, he addressed in the familiar, anything pressing for me in the next hour or so Betty? He knew there was not supposed to be. Ms. Brokaw always efficient did not have to bother her notes. Nothing for the next four hours boss. Good. If nothing pops up, then give me an hour or so undisturbed please? Betty Brokaw notes the time of her goldplated Speidel Twisoflex nodded. The warden entered again into his domain, quietly closed and latched the door, looked at himself in the very near future lying on his sofa of Corinthian leather and placed himself where he saw himself lying down stretch out to seconds ago.

Two days later.

Gaddammit you guys! You not gone believe who the fuck is in the Goddammit reception room!

It is pitch black at night. There is no moon out. There are thousands of white-like specks densely populating the clearness of the filament above mankind. That is or this particular small region of Earth's sparely populated real estate.

Why the actor Andy Griffith would come to ones mind is bleakly understood but it is of consequence.

One and a half days earlier.

It is a night of light rain drops. Even an hour of losing there heavenly obience to Earthly dewed grassy knolls aside expressway dampened asphalt roadways no hydroplaning nasceny applied.

The government vehicle cruise eastward only a few miles above the fifty five speed limit signs, posted the last forty miles.

The officers and their prisoner that was being transported back to penitentiary from his wife's funeral all were injured from the multiple three hundred eighty degree flips. The driver never saw the tire shredders placed in three path.

Stuned by crash no of the crashed vehicle ocopents were in any shape to stop themselves from being tranquilied by the darts.

Glenn Talbot, the prisoner never saw a face. The six of seven so he thought were all mask. Actually the four attackers had come for him, but when one of them put the head over his head effectively cutting off his sight he thought he was being kidnapped not freed.

Talbot was transferred to another auto. His hands loosely bound and he was uncuffed.

Why uncuff me? Came to a clearing mind a quarter hour later.

While sitting in the dirt at the bottom of an outward sloping knoll he cleared all questions. The guns no longer to his temples and the back of his head. He was sitting only a minute or so his thought patterns crystal sharp. I've been freed! His hands still bound loosely behind his back, it his him on the down to this spot I stopped on plenty of leaves and cracked twigs like the cereal. They on the other made no sounds. Special forces training. He was one. He knew. He freed his hands. The vest they had fit him with before binding him he thought had been filled with explosives.

The hood now off he cautious checked the four pockets on the vest. In the movies the pockets would have plastic explosive molded into bars. His pockets each had one hundred brands new one hundred dollar bills. Forty thousand dollars. Again he remembered. They made no sound leaving either. His head clear from the drugs from the dart. No confusion. Freedom was given him. Who did this?

It is amazing how quickly a country can turn on a President, by the country his own party affiliations are of concern.

The Headlines of Honor recipient mass murdered escapes.

It was this escape that removed Does Russia have weather making machine? From the networks, papers and talk shows. That was a justified headline considering the prison warden bowed to a presidential order to allow a convicted multi murderer to receive a guarded trip to the white house to have the well earned award granted. The escape took place hours after the inmates on furlow received the honor and was allowed his hands freed just long enough for the congratulatory shaking of commander in Chief's hand to be prepared for photo shopping.

The act was historical. The world was as a glutton. The president stepping in at the last moment before a convicted multi murdered was to received sentencing therefore staving off the death penalty.

Mack Moss was driving home from work. He had heard of the medal presenting ceremony over radio while checking the count of packages on the four feet by four feet wooden pallet. They were to be shipped by Lenzo Trucking to Setta Storage to awat overseas shipping. The count on this skid was correct.

This was the first time he had driven directly home from work without going to down a few cold ones in months.

Last night in bed he received a treat his first he hoped of many. Sex was not totally boring but after thirty five years of the same woman he had come to believe his sexual excitement was over – unless he began affair.

His wife Shirley must have been intuitive of his thought. The night before and all that day she ate verciforous vegetables. In the process of making love missionery style- Shirley Moss while her husband Mark was fully inside of her queefed.

Mark was doing a little more than just over the speed limit.

The Chevy thirty five hundred noticed the pedestrian. Sub consciously his mind and body demanding the quickest way home, so no giving rides to strangers. He drove on to his destination. He famished another last night which lasted into early morning.

Had he stopped to pick up the pedestrian than the phrase "Lucy I'm home." Would never been used by the escaped prisoner when on his own turned himself back in to the maximum holding facility.

Had he stopped to pick up the pedestrian he would have pushed the help call button on his armrest and On star would have sent police to his g.p.s. location. The manhunt would have ended with a forced capture rather than a self decided surrender.

Just prior to the Medal of Honor Awards Ceremony, the fifth member of the Belles hierarchy had been watching a weekly showing of a police story series. She finally said to her lesbian husband, these scenes where drowning cast members get to receive an c.p.r. always have disappointed me. Not one scene in hundreds of rescues when the water gushes out of them like geiser in the air is always purely clear water. None of them have had any sex? She inquires. She ends her dismay with, wheres the cum?

Her mate Esmerelda replies, I'll call Paramount and get Lucy Lee, right on it. Four minutes later, Lucy Esda! Hey!

CHAPTER FOUR

COVERAGE

The speaker of the House of Representatives approached the podium. She was absolutely resplendent in her dress designed by Finchi Mismhotept. She had chosen Rene Caovilla's flats, Misimhotept'a name sake partner. Her sun glasses designed by Solia Vargara.

Resulte on carrying a purse maintaining the full posture of femininity.

Her acceptance speech proudly laid out the role she now wore had once been partially carried though not officially sworn-in by the, great- the late, Mrs. Edith Bolling Galt Wilson wife of the most highly respected former President Thomas Woodrow Wilson.

A glance from her had only a short moment past gone to Chief Justice Larry Bucky Hill whom had administered the oath allowing her to take office. She did that while reporting on the kidnaping and relentless search for the vice-president. The president's assassination and the kidnapping both had eventuated the same day. Eventuated was the exact term she used for occurred. Her son Yendor, eight year old, fourth grader being home-schooled by his personal blonde haired, slimy figured creamy complexioned nanny-tutor governed his vocabulary and diction to place him stop his most elitest classes classmates, gave his mom that one as he had eavesdropped on her prepping for the acceptance oath's disquisition.

In her speech her mind not only buried the fast that she knew the vice-president would never again see the public, her mind mummified it.

In all she orated same seventeen minute and walked away with former president Richard Milhouse Nixon's infamous the two handed peace sing, as President of the United States of America.

That is all she could remember as she had been introduced, again by the Chief Justice Larry B Hill. This time though she was voted in by the electoral and the popular vote. A vast landslide read the Times, Sun and Post newspapers.

Thank you signs were stapled all over the city. Rumor was the Aryan Race group paid for them when she in her first term, the partial one, she had refused to allow the picture of a black female Harriet Tubman to be printed on the new twenty dollars bills.

Twenty two seats in the back of the chaimber were set aside for the Belles, a group well known in high society but the Belles did not attend inviting in their place two adult females and twenty preteen to teen young girls. The women both adorned small brimmed fancy red chapeau. The children's brims varied in style and size but all were pink in color. A thank you to them for the day two and a half years ago for bumping the Red Hat Societies gathering at the Platinum Ballroom.

The President's elocutional level was a magnanimous while silently invoking approbation to her new disquisition wordsmith one, Miss Susan Spencer. Who by the way receives two pay checks now.

The first two and half years of her term had may question why she had run for the office last term in the first place.

Inflation was nullified. Taxes reduced on the middle class by eleven percent. The national deficit decreased by three trillion dollars. Overseas policies and problems still remained the same, no worse Education now ejaculates a higher standard than ever in the past. Dentist finally got their due. Every American naturalized or "ripped-off from another country", her smiling phrase had the right to full dental coverage including microscopic whitening- roof canals dentures and or full implants and jaw bone rebuilding. Smiles justly seemed to pop-up all over the country. Leaders planet wide looked to her as a template as how a country should be led.

A short part of her speech went on the accolade trail noting she intended to stop child molestation, starting by giving a Presidential Pardon to a former Special Serviceman Medal of Honor winner serving multiple life sentences for taking the lives of three men who molested his daughter while he served over seas. Another citizens medal she intended to award to the become multi-billionaire for his two ideas, one saving the materials the US uses for paving streets and highways. A system using heat from auto and truck engines while driving to melt snow and ice: and the other making the US healthier by cleaning our citizens, a human washing machine.

These people she decided to award cause people over the planet realize America is doing it's part. She would use the platforms to increase an idea the inventor had given her on how to educate children to their highest possibilities and further educate all adults even those possessing multiple doctorates.

All parents must obtain the joyousness she had when her young son enhanced her first acceptance disquisition.

She would never say it aloud but her performance while in office had shown the exactness of former president Donald John Trump. She had with the overwhelming assistance and support of all political tory; the house, the Senate, the Congress and to some small extent the Supreme Cort, Justices made America Great Again.

One other law she had enforced over the commination of firing from one employment and jail time for not reporting even one transgretion of sexual misbehavior upon a stripling. Many school teachers, secretaries, nurses, principles, vice principles and crossing guards now realized not to have mistrust her words, child molestation must stop, for not reporting seen evidence of the child, misshapen mouths, bottoms, and tardiness were major evidence forcing surveillance of children's homes. Parents the single kind were given leeway only once as long as the perpetrator(s) were prosecuted along with parental testimony. No second chance was made very clear.

Welfare was and is being weaned out of existence. A parent on welfare had been given full warning via home visits. Should you have a child or children and you were a recipient, your next birthling should you choose to get in a condition cost were on you and so was an abortion. No more irresponsible pregnancies.

The world frowned and at home, the USA had massive protest rallies. The President with grandeur ignored them.

Governor's with the quickness of a cheetah got the message. Some made laws against rallying in order to stem off all would be violence. A few months transpired. The arguments ended.

The middle class soon after the elitest recognized one less minor inconvenience coming into being, up and coming, predestined, oncoming. God yes.

Still eyes were watching. Climpses of a more expansive profiteering future, leading with their guiding hands.

Four months into the future - That was one heck of movie. Our movies were no where near as entertaining and then there was no 3D. Her son had said that to the entire family. His youngest daughter Lynn Ellen, three and a half her legs spread wide open, one on either side of his ribs. His right forearm under her little flat bottom, his left arm in a ninety degree to his right supporting her back and maintaining the surely of a steady grip. She popping the third coconut toasted marshmallow in her father's mouth. Loralle was the second in age had a firm hold to her mother's ring finger hand. The grand mother walking next to and in a safe reach Ellen E. nine years old.

Walking back to the Rolls Royce limousine in the cubicled garage.

She was of two minds tonight. First and foremost which is the allocated designation of her decision is to cast her vote along with her compatriots, the rest of the Belle's elite five.

Until the decision was decided to fake the president's death and reassigning her with new identity rather than graciously memorializing after her would be assassination she would have voted with her mates though verbally giving her actual opinion. Her reason was carrying her younger granddaughter a few feet from her and going along stride for stride.

She carefully stifled the thought of personal dismay holding back the information- her paying cash money, one million dollars per man four in all totaling four million dollars military train to attack kill if ordered do whatever mission the were sent on and escape unscathed by her own hand to free that self same son well en route to his prison return from receiving the Medal of Honor from the president. He dismay at that time brought her to a few tears, an unusual occurrence for her and her kind by the way when she became enlightened of her sons self acquiescent return to his legalized place of confinement.

The daughter-in-law/wife/mother is now content. The warmth entering her tonight wore on his left hand ring finger the plain version the match if you will and even if you won't to the platinum band with six small diamonds in a white jade filigree carved pomegranate setting, must rare. The father to three girls and avenger to the children's impurity.

Back to the days after he returned himself in to prison.

Mentally the major thought, way to go soldier.

The lieutenant first class, said to himself, well I'll be a son of a crosseyed horny toad. He did it right.

The Colonel's surprise made him gleam showing his one gold tooth among a sea of a well cared for Pepsident smile. The pride he now felt he had never felt in thirty one years of armed forces service.

The last of the four another major said of the medal of honor winner but praising his parents, way to raise us one.

The End

CHARACTERS

Neighbor	Lawyer – Sam Wilson
Daughter	Jolene –
Son	Abet –
Father	Jo Hopscotch
Old case	Nest Alex – cold case cop devises TV show to get murder conviction against real estate sales woman on selling ghost house knowing ghosts possess it. Led to person's family and truck drivers death
Daughter and eldest	Dexeilia Abigel –
Youngest daughter	FN (short for allonym Fluffer Nutter)
Truck driver mother	Mrs. Hopscotch (Evelyn)
Mark Tuttte	
Aganess Bledsol	Head nurse Elaine Rothman Hospital
Merced	Aganness's Mom
Mrs Grossberger	Meredi's friezd since school
Udya Hopscotch	Truck driver
Xeilia Aba ail Hopscotch	Middle daughter
Sse eld	chief unsolved cases division
Nda Melicia inedict cold	Chief cold's wife
Josh White	
Arsette Missile White	Josh's wife
Theoleta Thompsun	state most attorney
Ann Bobby	partner most prestigious law firm

5 SOUTHERN BELLES

The Parson and his family of wife and nine young'uns were leaving their mansion for three days ownership in quite hurried fashion. The travelling home of six month. Rubber burned leaving traction marks some twenty yards into the parkway. Travel.

With pressing the electronic twenty feet gate barely gave way enough. The family was doing speed as though launched from a NASA launch pad. Still the closing gate left the auto's paint a scar in both driver's side doors and the right rear quarter panel. A broken red right turn signal covering would surely have an alert police traffic officer pull them over.

The conversation would go in this manner. Pulled you over for that broken tail light. Sorry officer. We were in a hurry. The security gate was closing to fast. That why the car looks keyed? Yes. License, ownership papers and insurance verification, all produced and verified an instance happened the police officer to ask a simple single question. That scratch on your side and the plastic pieces from your rear reflector still in the housing tells me this just happened what were you in such a hurry for. They driver and his passengers were then detained for a driving under the influence test. No argument was aroused. The minister had to agree to himself quietly that had he heard the reason for such a haste, had he been the traffic cop, he would conject a safety test would be in order. A tea tottler, non-smoker and no illegal narcotics user he had no problem passing the basic examinations. He passed the hand stretched out to touch his nose, the walking a straight line test and a breathilizer before being wished well and allowed on his way.

Maybe he is just insane. I got no test for that said the two striper after the family was only a few yards forward.

He gets on his squad cars radio. Car fifty four to car five. Come in Jake. Car five here. Go ahead fifty four here. Jake there's an orange family trailer.

There is the understanding many funerals umbrella are in use. Goes to movite most horrific unsurreal deaths occur on bright starlit nights as they do on beautiful sunny days. How is the weather were you are?

The chill told the r.v. driving preacher to drive the vehicle at full speed. He did so. Most drivers would have eased off the gas pedal when on a downhill droving highway. Not what happened. The result was the forty five foot dromonal Reo pulled trailer driver eyes met the preacher's.

The pieces of both vehicles....

The cold is intense. Renard the only boy child the preacher and his wife would ever parent in his sleep while dreaming of one of his future employment scenarios, on television the news reporter Smailliw luap was reporting on the tenth child to disappear this month was given a mental message from his agent, Renard "the preachers son" before I make you a superstar us, you and I make your not suffer the feeling of being beneath you. After all she is your mom. Naturally she will be proud of you anyway, but what if we make he famous, a communications superstar who gets the idea to help you with your career. Then we bring you up. Just below her status mind you.

Both Renard and he felt good with that. Both believing, maichistae, the reporter's mother received the mental communicate.

This type of career seemed to fulfill his awareness in his dream. One thing it had actually done was release. The fear from the haunted house he and his family are now fleeling.

Awakened fully aware of his surroundings, the cold showed him his real future the large vehicles collided one tenth of one second later.

On the same day as the pastor, his wife and children perished the short time of agony, of pain of crushed bones of pierchings and gasoline mingles diesel fuel blazing fire, the neighbor living next door to the tractor trailer driver drying in the same manner, only with her the diesel fuel mingled with the rv's gasoline her husband was being visited by Samuel the legal Eagle, Wilson.

Joe Hopscotch listened intently to his neighbor. And why should he not. Wilson had only yesterday won a verdict getting his client found not guilty for a murder where there were witnesses and camera videos showing his client in the act of taking the lives of three dark brown skinned women. The trial had been televised all over the planet.

That was not his first publicized win in such a manner. Lips and Brain, the legal equivalent to the most posh of magazine at the end of the case still in the courtroom gave Wilson his monogramed request letter to allow the magazine to award him lawyer of the year. It paid Wilson ten million dollars too.

Jolene Jobeth Hopscotch had to things done for her own behalf when summoned to the sitting room by her brother Abet.

J.J. Dad and Mister Wilson are in the chat room. Dad says for you to come in there immediately. He sounds solemn. Mister Wilson looks businesslike. What you did you can tell us later. Sounds important. Jolene turned off her Dell computer, she got from her wicker chair a mate to her desk. As she left her room Abet softly let a hand to her left shoulder. Be careful sis. Dad also told me to make sure none of us except you come in there until he gives us the nod. Abet knew his younger sister hung out with a crowd to be leery of. He went into his other two siblings bed room. Knock first Dipstick! Mildly shouting warned his next to youngest sister Jillette.

Jentile the youngest girl was at her desk studying where she might get the best exposure to boys her age that sold Skelcher light-up tennis foot wear.

The conversation took hours. Jousting back and fourth until the lawyer had completely explained, re-explained and again explained every aspect of the laws the Hopscotch child would have to face.

Finally the father and his daughter clearly knew avenue of the charges the common wealth would use to punish Joe Lene. The lawyer advice seemed best and mister Hopscotch decradled the land line, an old Victorian Cradle modle. He dialed nine one.

The police operator identified herself. Inquired what the emergency was and since being in that department for were a decade lended no shook in the caller turning his daughter in, she being one of students who attacked the old transient on the public subway train. The students face were covered due to COVID-19 public transit regulations. Operator six four nine seven dispatched the message over the radio to all patrol cars in the callers identified area.

Three and a half hours earlier a meeting began that ended in three and a half hours commenced.

You're going to need to know how to handle this. Did you see the news last night about the four school kids? You mean the one on the Uptown N train? The one the old hobo got attacked? Yes. That one. Man Jolene has a jacket exactly like one of the kids. Her shoe that the rider was beaten with. I've seen on your daughter a few times. Hell man she passes right in front of me everyday on her way to school. She's my next door neighbor. You're her father. Why didn't you notice it was your own daughter with those other thugs? Sooner or later, most likely sooner someone's going to not only recognize her as I did, but they're going to phone up the police. Get ahead of them. I'll help you. If you don't. Then I won't.

Joe Hopscotch viewed his son A out on the lawn. He tapped on the closed screen sliding door. His son's attention captured. Go get me Jolene, send her here immediately. Then you and your sister- do not bother us- unless it is serious.

Abet heads towards the stairs, yellow and green marbling on both sides of a thick Berricelli carpet. The staircase is six feet wide and the ornate pomegranate and bell filigreed silver inlaid baluster supports the twenty one foot long slightly curved alabaster coping.

J.J to her being verbally scolded, lectured and tutored. Those are the same stairs that lead.

The same stairway that would lead to her eventual freedom. Freedom from her participation from the heinious and violent crimes she did commit.

While Jolene listened intently the plan was laid out without a single insufficiency.

Neither she nor her co-harts faces were seen. She had assumed if none of her villians opened their mouth than no one would be able to catch them. She had too seen the video of their attacking the homeless guy on the news. Things appeared to her inexperienced self-cool.

What her now legal representative clearly opened her mind to was that all of the people the police would be searching for were school students getting or the train after school left out. Add to that her teachers would not only know one hundred percent what she wore to and from school that day but it is fairly believable some of her teachers would know who her girlfriends in school are. So would the goody-two-shoes classmates who saw them together every day. Closing out any discrepency that may have entered Jolene's mind Sam Wilson also knew her tight girlfriends and without doubt the four of the culprit girls names rolled of his tongue. She knew none of their faces were shown on the news reel. Her dad's condemning stare sealed it.

The lawyers cell phone rang. It was Frank Engel the former defendant of Wilson's second miracle non guilty verdict. The miracle in that case was Engel had no alibi. Engel had threatened the rapist of Danial O' Learhy, a nine year old curly red headed, fair skinned boy, Cameras had Engel in the area at the time of the killing. When all of that had surfaced, Engel gave a verbal confession and signed the written one on the dot-dot line. Denial is Frank's godson.

Engel's words came over the receiver. Good to hear from you man. Your last one hundred eighty eight thousand has just been deposited. I can never tell you how much I love you man. Laura is waiting. She says hey. The phone clicked.

The trio seaked in comfortable nine inch thick fast filled pillow seat cusions but only the lawyer felt at being in a modicum of ease. Jolene tense and ill at ease, gathered she was beated about the subway train incident yet a glimmer of hope.

Her father pissed off at his the thought of owning her choked in his brain. It did not expel.

Jolene's glimmer died. If you open your mouth even once until we tell you to I will fricassee your behind came from the man forcing himself to remember this meeting was to save his daughter, daughter came through that time and he did take it in that this was more than an attempt to reclaim his flesh and blood, from an arrest conviction, incarceration, possible lesbianism and a dead end future.

His face give no clue to the heat building up in him. He had by forced effort of his own taken notice of the young girls crotch as she first seated herself. Her yellow thong not even daring to try to keep court a fully hairy spread. She did not groom with a razor there. Both sides and the bottom of her underware had poured her vaginal crown outwards. Her legs folded under her now the picture remained. He went on with his legal barrage necessary to twart justice.

The police arrived at the front gate.

Officers Madello O'Brien and Blonten Zisk both took notice of a cell phone on the inside of table by the sitting room entrance. The two walked into the room at the behest of the man of the house. The lawyer and his client Jolene sat in silence.

On the stairway leading to the bedroom are the other three offspring. As in his training officer Zisk glances the blind spots from the front door until he has entered the sitting room. He did take full notice of the children. During the briefing given them he almost completely forgot about them. Neither the father nor the two city cops even gave a seconds thought to the cell phone on the table. The phone still recording every word.

So much is going on downstairs it is all but impossible having attention on the three young one upstairs. The two older Abet and Dexeilia Abigai sit in that joining are a where the upper hallway meets the crowning step, gathering difficulty. Dexeillia asks her older brother what is the name of the area where they sat. What area? She explained. The place where the hallway meets the top tied running her finger on the marble tied and the panels, touching again with her finger both sides of the marble panels and finally with her pointer finger the carpeted riser step.

His genius mind and teaching part click in. He decides not to pull one over on her. Not this time. Best to stay serious with the goings on down stairs. A short answer, the American languages has none. Please hold on to anything else until we know what is the conclusion pointing downstairs.

The youngest has now joined them. She informs them Buster's kidnapped. Mrs. Millen on the news just reported the story. Proud of using the phrase just reported rather than just said. Who stole him wants ten million dollars or before thanksgiving or they are going to eat him. The kidnapped Buster's is the name of the Thanksgiving bird reprieved via presidential pardon. It had been on its way to Disney world to preside over the holiday's parade.

Abet paid almost no attention to his turkey caring sister. Then the thought could CIA security have just been tested? And failed.

Officers sit down this is going to take a bit of explaining came his father's voice from the family meeting room.

Picturing the news report, I hereby pardon you Buster's you are now free from being thanksgiving day's main course. The picture lingered as he had viewed the report on his bedroom one hundred inch projected on the ceiling. Though crossed his mind, have all pardon turkeys over the years been white.

As young as he was he could not expel the exam in his head. If black lives matters came from an anti racist view point then why did we, most Americans being we celebrate this most racist of occasions.

Country western music could not even have saved the original inhabitants, so the joke goes.

His minds sharpness was attacked so numerous of times with those last few thoughts. Good thing I am recording the conversation downstairs.

Jolene had missed nothing. She was ripped up inside. Hold back the tears. Do not hold my niagra. Her visage on her face too was adorned. Wicked confliction.

Sorrow depressed her and her face hid the rest of her tears in her brothers pajama shirt pocket beginning the wetness. Seconds ago one of droplets left her right eye ball abandoning the others. The tear had for a short time plenty of companions first the lower eyelid it swelled up behind rolled over the edge. It met a few short curvy eyelashes, the out part of that eyelid rolling down it to the upper part of the skin on a high cheek bone. The moist droplet bred by sadness, worry and fear might have traveled the full of her jaw but for her chin resting on her clavicle. All those parts kept the salt water company until it took the lonely fall from her cheek highlighted by the hallways two fluorescent lights, one in yellow the other in pale pink. Their mother's design for when she was way for days up to a week doing her job.

The loneliness desisted on the ninety five percent cotton, five percent polyester night gown in dinosaur picturesque boutique. Just above her knee recognized the moisture after the materials saturation. Her face sank to Abet's chest for comfort from the words of the talkative adults below on the first floor of house, her home. The flood came quietly muffled by her siblings garment.

For the first time since alighting and ease dropping she did not hear the voices.

Abet and petite FN however heard it. FN's slight head jerk aligned with her quizzical look on her face alerted her big brother that at some time in the near future he may have to explain the lawyers articulation as her father went to answer the front doors chiming. Tell no one, said quietly but with a guiding forcefulness married to it, except the judge while you are on trial that you are not sorry for what you did, but you are aware that you should be for doing someone wrong and that you are working on becoming a better female so that you will recognize that you are sorry. I guarantee you no prison time. After the police came in from entering the front door with there father Jolene did exactly as the three of them had her rehearse. She never said a word and she could have won an Emmy with the I am so so sorry face. Her eyes even reddened and watered. Which may have been realization and regret. Police on some occasions rub people in such a manner.

Comforting can be done the same as getting comforted with no awareness on ones body movements. Somehow that sounds incorrect if as reported by thousands of neurological scientists conclusion the brain controls the body's movement.

Abet's wet loosely buttoned pajama bottoms cratch now has his sobbling tearful sister's full frontal face weeping with slight spasms in direct contant. Gravity doing its part. Jolene remains crumpled Abet's left arm on her shoulder and back. FN's little face and her low sprine both arms crabling a hip, not yet able to circumference.

Downstairs the performance, briefed as she was was of epic proportion. The script, her briefing given to her by the award winning attorney deserved an Oscar for best writer of a daytime drama. He put it together before the sun went down. He only delayed until Jolene's dad came in from work. Even the part where he told Jolene of the speech for the judge only when her father went to the door to let in the local authorities.

Fluffer Nutter looked so innocently beautiful carry to find who it was her sister victimized and when she got bigger should she beat the girl up too.

Sam Wilson had previously found the D.A.'s telephone number assigned to the violent attackers should their names evolve in order for their prosecution. The two, Silson and Al Flemming the D.A. agreed to meet at the precinct to meet the surrenderee and her attorney, being as how his secretary was somehow informed by him to alert the news crews. All the stations agreed. I'll have a camera crew there in a few shakes. The arrest at the precinct was agreed to be ten minutes later than necessary. The camera crews. The D.A.'s publicity coverage. And Sam Wilson superstar lawyer. Promotion gleamed in the emerald spectators of Flemming.

Jolene had been so preoccupied with contain and maintaining legal directions she had neglected to keep track of time, although earlier in day after returning home from school she remember to detract but at that time decided to delay the pads assertion blocking her soon to flowing vagina's crimson tide.

It did happen in the patrol car. She alerted officer Rechiel, the driver. He in turned radioed the station, through her he attained her lawyers phone number. The cause was approved by the station's supervisor. The corporal phoned Sam Wilson, her attorney and given the proper instructions, he stopped by Rite-Aid.

When the came came through Sam Wilson had just a second or to before heard the sweetness of Sharon Davis. His Brain betrayed present day reality. The sweetness went from hears to his nostrils. He wafted his mind in her frankencense. Sharon Davis the nineteen year old ten thousand dollar a right prostitute. The in crowd knows. She will mayor next election.

Sex is always one of his highest adjudicators. However his clients are always without restriction save for his own being and God above, above him, paramount.

He tapped the security guard on the left uniformed hip. Keep your eyes on me the University Corporation guard was told. The culprit had not came near the Rite – Aid exit yet. Waiting in line with the box of comfort inside maxi pads, he loudly sneezed and asserted his way into cashier's guards and three others attention. When the candy thief tried to exit the lawyer caught the security guards eye and with outwardly deliberateness nodded his his forehead towards the thief.

The fight was short.

Before leaving Wilson turned from the checkout counter retrieve Cadbury Caramellos. The candy bars cost alone he knew would be over three dollars along with the pads eight dollars and some change came back from his Jackson.

He changed his thought from using his T.D. Bank debit card. He did not relish the box of feminine pads on his statement. He is a bachelor and he has no children.

The event of the caught and handcuffed candy thief behind him he left the drug store.

As though the sound of a Dick Wolf created television shows, Law and Order Special Victims unit theme music caresses his mind, it appears most of the people in the city realizes it's entertainment value.

As sharp and as intelligent a lawyer should maybe comprehend, the theme music is from a series dealing with the catching and convictions of rapist attached to justice for the victims unwanted attachments. Now with the reporting and apprehension of a confections purloiner.

His country western music fettish takes a hold of his radio. Not in Boise. Nor even in Idoho. Still his cars adhere to KISSIN is in both Boise and Idaho. Ahhhh! Rodeo. Ahhh! It's the country studio Crew Jammin on Garth Brooks. He commencerates the song flattening the ahhhs. Rodeo, Garth Brooks.

He does not complete his listening to his habitual glee. He has arrived. The thunder Rolls but for Jolene he squelches his delectable.

Without having to gather his breath, he unlocks the driver's side door with verbal command driver's side front door unlock.

Scantily clad see through side on bouses and slacks she guides the female prevent through the prisoner's entrance door on the side of the building.

Leaving the side parking lot Wilson traversed the two flights of steps. Each had no more nor no less than four stoney entrenched hard cement steps.

The fragrance of orchard like, lily and lilac floral fragrance hit him immediately as his first leg entered the thirty seventh precinct's entrance way. His approval was commanded. The opulence of the aromatic air aside I am Mister Sam Wilson attorney. I am here to represent Miss Jolene Hopscotch hoping the Miss rather than Ms. did not catch the train that rolls right over their bridge. Bridge an allonym for head, reminding the officers Jolene is still a young child. No matter the charge. Future planning? His thought forced a denial of the present sometimes influenced the future. He was led to the precinct supervisor.

The corporal's visage. Sloppy. Shoes unshined. No neck tie. Holster has seen for better days. Still, perhaps a future Serpico. The seventeen ribbons decorating his uniform blouse was the only clue. Then came clincher. Those blue-white eye balls green crystalline eyes with a few flecks of Caucasian brindling. They actual sparkled. A longer momentary settling of light in them and they glistened. Even the eye-ball blue. This man is sharp.

Give me a moment said the corporal. I try to always be ready and at my best. But I going for my p.h.d. and my dumb self chose a thesis that is almost impossible to document, evidence. Wilson already having two phd's his interest somewhat piqued, what is it? Your thesis I mean. The supervisor's reply comes. I chose this one, in the venerable words of former president John Fitzgerald, Kennedy, not because it's easy, but because it's hard.

I titled it are all newborn girls vagina's at thee integument the same shape or does having penile penetration cause a diversities along the way?

The corporal elaborated, getting around on the internet, scheeech. The FBI's.

Very little if at any time in the past has Sam Wilson been truly stymied. He thought. Stumped to stage of embarrassment until his calling brought him back. There it was, Jolene, Jolene. The words that finally came out of his mouth, whoo, good luck with that.

I am not sleepy. F.N. was getting on a huge anry. Determined to stay diligent until her family was all home and waiting for mommy to come home from work.

Her devotion even for such a young one untainted by let downs augments and disappointments of others. Reward surely must wait for her in the near future and the distant one the same.

Three minutes later her first reward arrived. It arrived on the tide of time and the softness and comfort in the middle of stuffed couch so lenient the bossoms of Dolly Parton would take a distant second, such could only lead to quiet, soft breathing, slumber with a silent sigh straight into dreamland. The soon to be oncoming dream would become one of her most warm hearted favorites. This one she saved her presidents life along the whole CIA and their wives and children.

She came only with the recipe and made the bomb equivalent to the West Buster, Spain's newest bomb to scare the USA into buying toys broke real, really easy and had no refunds and no exchange.

Her bomb, boys "R" Yucky, was made of dish washer rinse water, the extra large carogated tube of cleanser, a hidable detonator and the left eye of Abet's mosest favorite G.I. gorilla doll. Even if Abet used to argue with her the toy is not a doll fluffer Mutter. It is an action figure.

Somewhere in her dream in a mist, a cloud making it invisible to dis-earn was a figure unable to view by any except FU was a slyly smiling almost seeable face, seeable only to FN mouthing quietly, understandable to her only, an action figure with only one eye. And her own mind. I bet you won't only leave me one elegant with yellow icinged drum on his back next county Fair day.

Hmmm, as she self assuredly rolled from her side to full out prone position on flat lying frontal body. Except for that one left leg. Every time she slept so smugly that left knee was always bent in a hundred an ten degree angle. Knee touching her left almost fisted a little world saving hand. One and only one fingernail painted. Mom wasn't home. Only mommy paints all my nails. Just little Daddy only let her point his nales. When she is awake and not dreaming of course.

An aspect of reality had with notice invaded dreamland asserting no warning, no awareness what-so-ever of in pending doom a change in life, one unwanted, one feared and although it first appeared in her sleep, the quiet bell soon of awakening creepily, silently extols and evlogizes, soon, soon soon.

As was their custom when spending a week or so with the grands the little ones both boys bestrum three and the eldes Benedict almost five never knocked on a closed door. The huge double master bedroom was also included in their youthful disdain of all privacy. Super here strength a Herculeen feet to Steve Reeves the double obstruction.

When the doors opened grandpa sat at the bed's end shirtless Grandma aware of her heirs, heirs procliuities never missed a strake and truth be told only minimally did her neck and head rhythm decrease their proclivity at opening any door unannounced having been well gotten used. The grandes visited much as mom a huge movie director and dad usually mom's executive producer and off times special Guest Star took great precautions with their offspring in today's unnatural desires for young children. Thus the grandparents. The least expensive best child caretakers on this here Earth.

The air coded comforter fully camoflagued grandma on the Louis Vuitton pillows cradling her two naked knees. Grandma's dishabille on the carpet. Her nudite still opaqued.

The seventy two year old woman defif the effigy of time. There was only one female whose crowing glory match the figure now servicing mate of fifty one years. She was now off directing Hollywoods latest blockbuster soon to be.

She and four others in her field have the strangling Hollywood now gasping for air rather than as it had been, unconscious from the former land grabbing Japanese which had the city all but called dead and autopsied. Perhaps some payback for the internment of World War 2.

Just think. Somewhere someones man, wife daughter someones loved one anyway ain't comin home tonight. Go on home. Kiss peg and Bob. They might not know but you do. So be damn glad for them that you can go home, and a family to go home to.

Men do often look in one another's eyes. This is one of those times when an I'll see you tomorrow can shut down a conversation. While in his minds forefront his commander also thinks but keeps his thoughts checked.

As his workmate drives off. Away. Home. Sure going home to Peg is a good thing. Why do the two of you taint it with a third. Your ass is spreading. And your lips show just how wide that dick is you and Peg have been sucking. What happened to the good de days when America was a one nation under Gods country. He now departs home to house with a college grand and the grads son and daughter (he smiles genuinely) and his daughter-in-law about to cash in the multi mil lottery. Yeah! He smiles. Didactically. The curse of a caring human being stifled a true jubilation. For no apparent reason his brain is haunted by the television episode. Put a sardine in the postal slot and drop it on the saucer for my... he dumps everything else and there is vision of his anguish destroyer. A two story Greek revival and seven bedrooms. Not attempting to solve the puzzle, he satisfies his savage breast. Somewhere in there. There is home. Protest is home, waiting is dinner. Longing is protest. If you would seek him now, forget about it, you probably with global tensions, political unrest and racial violent outbreaks have more enemy's than you care to have. Leave him with her and the children, you may have a friend.

Mark Tuttle was about to head on back to his room. He hissed his finger and lightly pressed it against Aganess's forehead. Without having to look she gave her good feeling sense of approval.

Aganess the head nurse of Pennsville Rothman and Elaine Rothman Hospital had been on duty those nineteen some odd years ago when Mark's mom puttered Mark on out of there. Seven pounds exact. She has loved and help raise that boy eversince. Hey Mark! She calls as he waits for the up elevator. Bite me!! She finishes. For now. She will give her sometime the detail tomorrow.

The elevator indicator lights up. Up. He sends as acknowledging pointer finger and a sideways glance.

Aganess has a youthful way of giving an invite to eat. Aganess Bledsce's plates at the county have had to increase in number of plates for the last fifteen county fairs.

Even old Mrs. Grossenbet had to give way to Aganess's cooking. It had been that way every since Mercedi, Aganess's mother and Mrs. Grossenbet's closest ally since grade school. Secretly all the other women loved Aganess though few would admit why. On county fair weekend no matter how they and your man were getting along, should one wait he soon would be found at Aganess's table.

The couple had purchased the doorbell at Walmart's Department Store before the first of the four children were born. It was advertised in the store. The Hopscotch did know it was a true item. A television show used the idea of it as a comedic foil.

He was so elated he had it. She was demurely pleased her hardworking, loving husband had a new and useful long lasting toy. She enjoyed it best on let's pretend night. He stayed in form. Feigning to have forgotten his front door key, usually it was still on the ring with those of the Volvo.

He would savor pushing the button. While on the inside before the children she gave herself leave way to question, who could that be when hearing the someone's at the door called out by the mechanical device.

All these years later she still helped keep her mind young and active.

She never allowed her mind to allow the answer to the question whom it could be in her house telling her someones at the door.

Over the years she silently congratulated herself for her earnest all out commitment of denying the door's voice as a mechanical device even when she realized one after the other of children learned vocalization.

Her presence is always anticipated when she was on the road. He presence is missing now- heavily.

Jolene showered, said her prayers and looked in on her siblings, then went to bed.

Okay man. Your children are all in tight, what do want. Why did you ask me to wait?

I watched the news while you represented Jolene at the precinct. Just as said the reporters put you on. My family had two bulletins on the show. Jolene's and Evelyn's. Evelyn's come the lawyer's questioning response to Jo Hopscotch Evelyn's gone. Her semi crashed head on into a family camper. She's gone.

The detectives called me first, before the broadcast hit the sorene. She is dead Jo Hopscotch heart was in his eyes. There, waiting to be alone was Niagra Falls.

Dexeilia Abigail is the middle daughter. Until the call came she had fallen asleep. Someone at the door. Dexeilia drowsily shook he head. She came to the top staircase and made a start downwards. She saw her father finger Sam Wilson into silence. Being discovered barely, slightly took a glance at her, still, she waited.

The Chief of Unsolved Cases Divion, Two star, General Cold, Case sat at home his legs crossed just above the thin as tooth pick sized ankels and on the Ashati Stool hassack sized lighted the flat of his palm on the enormous volumned buttocks of Linda Melicia Benedict Cold, his, you can use another cold one smiling spouse.

PREVERT — PART 1

CHAPTER ONE

SHAHADI

The doggone turncoat wouldn't do what was supposed to be done. I found out over the few trials initiated according to advertisement and the belief in the way things are supposed to go will be the way things go. Explicably the finks who sold me on the idea of how this was going to end must have known to handle the situation was in most certainty would ill cause the advertised desired effect.

Your honor what price can a man put on the negative attainment of piece of steady orim. Yooo honor, surely you have taken a mental note on how I now am despicably referring to what if obtained then I would be referring to it as an easy ongoing slice of heaven. Also had the item performed as promise than I would not be gracing your presence here today taking up the commonwealth's costly time.

My soon to be would have been paid for partial evenings paid entertainment extricated herself with the quickness of the beginning of a lightning bolt's flash.

Thankfully she left without allotting on my even a singular solitary expletive allonym.

Since I rent a furnished and accompanying private bath on the second floor in a two story brick fully attached, another house on either side, row of houses of the same sorted manner I did walk her down the stairs to allow her dismissal.

Watching that still clothed unpenised ass walk out was torment. Mea some the torment as high on the scale of mental anguish as the height of expected pleasure was when she and I came to a harmonized concordance of the terms for her to accept my partaking as I am sure due to it's softness, it's curvature and it's all around delightful feeling grievance, did those before me.

Before I closed the door I made a sweep the few leaves from the porch with the outside broom and plastics snow shovel in the kitchen. Hmmm, I thought. Still before heading inside and shutting the front door I lean forward. I take on step with my right foot. It lands on the porch as I try to catch a last sighting. I don't have to tell you of what no use. She has crossed to the other side of the street too many parked cars. Guess I'll have to be a thief tonight. Piercing my thought is my left hand. Without putting work to eat, my right quietly but with the force of a knockout punch affirms it's authority, the doors both closed. Iron storm and steal entry. The entry door usually does as it did old at ajar. I press it easily and hear the low thump against the frame. Then the click. The click is it securing.

Looking upwards the two doors locked and closed I remember two things, the trek down them a minute or so ago and there are fifteen of them.

The Christmas stocking is off the door. I see that as my foot lands on the top stop. The toilet is behind the door on my right. It's key is on the ring along with the down stairs front door and the bedroom just in front of my eyes where the boot with the white trimmed top no longer is taped. This string white blinking lights I had taped to the commode and along the sides and top of the window and down. I cannot see that they are down through the locked white painted door but since I am the one took them down. I know.

Before I put the key into the bedroom's door lock to unlock it a mental note brief but precise and crystal clear clarity is the delineation. The wealthiest business part of sixth largest city in the country are on the side, small streets, heavily travelled during business hours are three homeless shanty types of homeless residents, I prescribe residents for lack of a definition of higher quality, two have bedding for couples, one a young man and a young female, the second female and male both senior citizens and one of flattened corrugated refrigerator and oven boxes for a single guy.

Once I enter through this door, the homelessness does not apply but still just as that bum sleeping in the streets through I guess all sorts of weather, I am a single guy.

When the time arrives that usually does I will remember which of these trouser pockets has the key in my left cargo pocket. The door opens. I retract the key. There is where moments ago my boredom would have been prohibited. Temporarily. Better than unceasing continuous I gather. The mattress is no longer lonely. It has me again. Me and me only thanks to you. Thanks to it. I see the numerous traps on the carpet. There are empty. As usual.

You lousey little version of a rat. Evolution has smartened you. It has been months since I set them. You go near them and then not follow the true course of the plans. You divert and go around them. Time and some kind of transference of knowledge from former and unwisened. Members of your species that died in them prevent you from following their suit. They are dead. Neck bones snapped in half.

Why did you have to be the one their knowledge diverged into.

My manhood limp and lonely, longing is the way it is. She came in this room. You made an unnecessary appearance and that was all she wrote.

Thinking of getting a cat. Would you avoid the feline? If not safety would dictate I get rid of purring predator as soon as the contractoral hit has taken place. Leaving her alone in here with a natural tongue-bad ideas.

His prick stiffened. It had started when she earlier she had fucked the producer, sucked the writer's ass, balls and dick. The film director put a frilly woman's thigh high plastic apron her. On her knees she sucked each of their hard cocks finishing one before starting the second and then the third. Each of them after cumming in her mouth held her head in place on his dick until she drank the full shorting of his piss. She then gave each a second blowjob better than the first. She was now ready for the two stars of the movie to come in to eat and mount her asshole. Her asshole really needed have been paid more attention to with soap, water, washcloth and the necessary time and motion to keep away the dark discoloration from not doing so over goodly amount of years.

It had been filmed from her coming through the door way until an hour went by awaiting the two stars.

The doorbell rang. I know you perceived it's sound. Ding dong, ding dong. The stars are here. They await entry on the front porch.

Pleasantries and instignations have been exchanged. Shots of tequila and lime go to all with the exception of the two canines, one eighteen month greyhound male, slimgoody. The Saluki, a close look alike of the greyhound yet smaller female is twelve and a half months old. Her name is Little Lotta.

The script has been read and all the humans have their indication of acceptance of terms. The woman who arrived earlier and performed for the movies officials agrees to eight thousand dollars for a forty five minute performance including her earlier taping.

The two males, owners of the two animals receive two thousand dollars. One thousand for each of them.

The cameras roll. The canines go into their routine. It was so well done all who see this movie will be sure the animals were trained together for their performance.

Until that day the thought of a dog licking its private area was a commonality, but the female gave Slimgoody the most loving tender blowjob ever seen. Human women on the most part would have taken notes. There would be no such word as a break-up. No way one's husband would conceive of allowing his wife to divorce should their marriage routine engulf her way of having the greyhound male moving and feeling the greyhound's every shiver and quiver. Halting at times to muscle tensing and tightening spasmatic seizorelike euphorical but deadly silent Little Lotta's tongue laying over the side of as mandibular incisors goo slopping the makeshift bedding.

Act one and act accomplished. Both are wraps sounded the director. Take a break. Last act setting. Get it done. We shoot in thirty five.

Clarity. I am dreaming. Knowing before I do it, it is a bad idea. Human frailty. I do it.

My windows are secured. Both in a different manner. The television partly obscures the window facing the bed. It is in lock position. The other is fastened to the air conditioner not in use. It is December thirty first, my stupid ego said to do, so I did. I rolled from my flat lying position to my left side. A semi fetal position. Left arm under the side of my head, right arm across my ribs. Here comes the part where my stupidity reigns king over my mind and to a sadder, sorer outcome. My arthritis is in such a state that I need a hip replacement. No, I do not roll on the arthritic hips though in the past... my stupidity, my right leg overlaps my left. I am in that semi-fetal position I brought to you a short bit back, legs angled about fifty five percent. The condition is progressed it will have a story to tell when I try to turn over again on my back. Really does not matter the legs over lapping, because any sideways position while lying down lends to the phrase, wounded in action. Is here a good time to enlighten you that just before rolling off my back to my side a short state of hypnopompia occurred. Once on my side a state of hypnagogia occurred.

My next set of rapid eye movements first few seconds of all things showed me an advertisement of all things. I did not get it all but what did take a hold to me were two bits of information. Important bits I postulate. Artificial intelligence disruptor was the lesser of the important. Two names Jeff Bezos was one Elon Musk the other. I did not hear the que, lights. Nor the first letter in camera but only camera action.

The male Slimgoody had mounted the female in a missionary position and Little Lotta hold onto her rhythmic humper as though in rhapsodic ecstacy. Both her rear legs wrapped around his anched hips the toes of her paws curled like overbaked cheese curls. Her front left leg was under his right one paw nails sank into his ribs. Her left front leg was wrapped tighter than a cap on a jar of preserves around and stop his left foreleg shoulder, paw clawed into his slim racer neck. Uuvvvuhhuuhh was so soft you could barely decipher the sound.

When she came, somehow the professional in her would not let him go with her.

You could tell the greyhound was a bit angry as he withdrew from her vuluz. I guess hats why he rammed hard, fast and fully right past her perineum and into her butt. That did it. She still did want to let him free of her four legged fetter, but his once two toned striped like notted dog lipstick, had gone limp and fallen out.

She was by way of hand signal directed to approach the part of the set about to be filmed. Little Lotta had rolled over on to her side. The woman kneeled, lifted Lotta's thin haired tail revealing the premium and put her face directly under the tail. The woman began with a forefinger rub, lightly, gently, slowly crossing it. A pucker at the butt appeared. Open, close. Open, close. Open, close. The human woman's tongue parted it's teeth, then it's lips. Her eyes never waivered. Her mouth was wet. As the human woman's tongue approached the pucking hole a loud thump aroused all of movie people inside the room. The front door opened via violence. The batterer was as yet not seem. Vice! Was yelled out loudly and thirteen officers of the law caused the motion picture porn people to be transfixed. The dogs showed more amazement then did the human participants.

Looking directly into the officers faces, some in uniform, Brenda Karen, the name of the female whose hands now held Little Lotta motionless quickly flicked two licks to the surface of Lotta's pernium and then jabbed Lotta's butt hole with a roled up tongue point.

Though the cameraman had also frozen in posture the camera recording light still remained red, transfixed. It caught the vice police officer's forced entry but it missed recording the scene which would if entered into the AVN Oscars nomination had been a shoe in to win.

All the video participant in hand cuffs their rights read to them, Sargeaht Lopez, not in uniform here but heavily decorated when in his dress uniforms ask his fellow vice squad officer, another highly decorated officer, but also not in uniform here, Jeff what do you call a frozen Russian cop? Jeff Peterman hears but never answers Lopez's riddles. Lopez gives the Peterman the rejoinder. A hammer and popcycle. Lopez gets no response O.K. O.K. so it's not great but it was good to be in a harbinger movie.

Governor Burgeous Brentmeier's office received only one top secure message that day. The Welter Code was set up by the governor himself. He only know how to decipher that type of message. The cipher was given to only one man, Hewlitt Redmond.

Redmond sent it. Alone with his security and his sectary walking the mansion to the lunch hall he opened and read it. After reading he did not take another step.

Excuse me everyone he said. This matter is marked urgent answer now. You guys go on to lunch. Lem, Lemulle Arther, the governor's secretary, cancel everything until I call you. The governor headed towards the elevator, entered the garage and took Lem's Audi.

That governor's analytical mind has clicked in. He knows he needs to get a message to Hewlitte Redmond. One where it will not seem off to anyone. He had never used this vehicle of communication before yet it has been prepared for use. He heads to L street.

The date is there. The date has never seen this Audi before. As a

Cherkee van approaches Shahadi he side to its rear gets out of the Audi and beeps his horn. Shahadi looks. Sees him, waves of the van and gets into the Audi's passenger door.

Shahadi first removing the yellow lipstick, then goes directly work. He is out of his slightly pulled down suit trousers and her mouth engulfs his fullness. Tounging his nuts while sucking his stiff nine and three quarter inches. Shahadi personally has damn near thickened him by a third of his circumference and added an inch to his length over the past six years. Meant to order. The date is unaceostomed to his use of the phone while driving her around the D.C.'s Olympia area but it really doesn't matter.

He has gotten his coded message to his daughter's private detective paid to follow her.

Three hundred dollars and one hour of pleasuring later Shahadi is dropped off.

No one knows who is not a customer of Shahadi and the body is a deep dark people, blue black smooth as silk skin to a twenty six years old male born Alexander Ryder the Fourth.

CHAPTER TWO

PEGANTHA BUNDY MARTIN

Sergeant detective Martin chocked todays arrest one last time clocked out and drove to Henry's the local police tavern in his police district's area. His constitution usually was to order a double Tanqueray, Pat Roscha on her flat bottom, leave a fiver for her keep her mouth shut about his hand tap in the crack of her flat ass tip then go home to his loving though infadelous wife of forty years Pegantha Bundy Martin.

While in the one hundred first precinct Martin's clocking out has changed the mood of the lecherous criminals wearing the badges of legal employees of Washington D.C's police both patrolman, supervisors and detectives.

Brenda Karen is unknown has never sought the general populations notice none of the police know she is the governor's daughter. Brenda gives no statement to be written down. When the officers hear of the course of her arrest she is visited in the back jail's cell often by both male and female police. All are orally and or vaginally and or anally serviced by her. She was left no choice by any of them.

With the eleven men and women on duty and not on the streets finished for some of their first time with Heg Peg had not once orgasmed nor did she even attain a steady wetness.

A fat Caucasian female corporal with the award colorful ribbons over her uniform blouse pocket went in the cell pulled down her slacks and presented her back side new peg. A really slobbery asshole licking took place. The woman's anus hole locked ten shades darker than the buttocks surrounding it. She literally needed to wash her ass longer than the time she had been taking if she washed her rectum at all. Her as stank like shit warmed over.

Said during the forced oral to anal rape you're gonna eat my ass until I shit or I run out farts. Pegantha had tears rolling. Her pride broken. All she could now come up with was I refused to think dad help me.

Had she not still had her hands cuffed behind and a second set of cuffs locked the pair on her wrist to the metal bench she proclaimed I would kick your ass.

The chop turned around and punched Pegantha in the eye as hard as she could. The lid split and blood poured down the side of her face.

At each of the pornographic movie makers arrangement minor charges where up held and minimal bails were posted. Since no law existed on animal porn the greyhound and saluki were return to their owners.

Curious to some but not to many men the little Lotta had returned home. She was feed and watered. She got into a large shower with her owner and she was being shampooed her lather was so thick and rich her owner lifted her scratched her head through the luxurious peach cobler aromaed foam turned the dogs face towards the running water from the star shaped gold brass colored shower head. Lotta made low yelp for a couple of seconds, as her owner ran his stiff ramrod into her doggie cunt.

Pajabi Cusnari, a female of Angolan decent had turned out to be a slimy slut there is no wondering why as she was raised by her mother and her mother's numerous sex pieces who had lived in the apartment an average two or three weeks each and only seemed to be replaced by another accordance to his or her selves after Pujari had sexually molested and rarely as a child was she bathed thus she still carried a dark skinned completion died into her over the years of her being an object of misuse.

She somewhere along the way to her adulthood filthy mind, filthy both, foul attitude had gelled into her personal behaviors. She was a bit thrifty. She waited until her hair spray was empty before she opened the bottle removing the spray nozzle putting in it a little: hair grease: a little oleo: some of her urine: a little water: and last but the filthiest of all while she had sat on her commode in her bathroom eliviating her person of it's solod waste, that little piece that always seem to linger just inside her asshole she put the spray bottle's opening just below her asshole and fired into the plastic bottle that last little piece of shit.

After replacing the sprayer part she placed the plastic cylinder like top back in place holding the top tight shook the container, then she put it in her purse. Hundreds of other slimy, nasty ass citizens had been effecting the same sort of misbehavioral characteristics.

She had taken a private taxi service, the unadvertising their company kind. The taxi driver pulled up and parked at the front door of the apartment building she had requested. The uniformed doorman walked briskly with a struct uncommon to that of the United States air force and opened the now unlocked near passenger door.

The driver showed only a slightness of surprise as the door said, good evening Miss Karen. She did reply. The door man structed again, this time to open the door for her entrance.

The governor's daughter proceeded to the fourteenth floor and entered her two point four million dollar flat. Ruffus met her with a what took you so long to get home. It is good to see you. You okay?

I am finished, look.

Two short years ago before her life changing epiphany when she would get into her shower it would going their along with her. Lately a smirk like smile accompanied her.

She purposefully left the lavatory door open. She delighted in watching her Doberman, ruffus eat. She made certain a quart of fresh carbonated unflavored water was in his water dish. Ruffus is an extremely rare animal with the disease of luecism. Other than his albinoism he was one of the healthiest animals alive. Very well groomed too.

She either needed the extra time to clear her head mind she enjoyed a long time taken to wash her small pink nipples later that day the female police officer sat with two of her vice card colleagues. She was having bourbon neat and an ale light. Not one person other the perpetrator noticed the black women walk in and go in directly to the ladies room. In a stall her purse was opened an a plastic bottle with a plastic top was removed. Removed also was an empty small plastic eye wash aerosol container. She filled the little eye was spray container with a small amount of a dark looking liquidic concoction and recapped both the containers. On her way out her jacket covered her forearm and hand. The hand carried the smaller container and as toilet user went on her way back out of bar she left by way of going out behind the female officer who had raped Brenda in the precinct cell earlier and sprayed the mist twice in the back of the police officer new hair do. She exited.

Karma may have had a little to do with a incident. The toilet user had never even heard of Brenda Karen. Truth be told, she would not know Brenda Karen from a whole in the ground.

Sergeant detective Martin pulled into the drive way. It had been repaved and stone set in the still hot eight inches of asphalt. His wife saw lights go dark as returned in the paved entrance. He pushed remote on his key fob and the motorized garage door began to go up.

While the door was going up, so did his wife's yellow polka-dotted thong. She had showed away bless it the families cat, a hairless sphynx who had just been enjoying a second a oiled sardine from the anus pore of the now home detective Sergeant wife Pegantha. Pegantha had already came twenty minutes ago from rubbing her extra large sized man dick otherwise called a big clit and Bless it intermittently licking between her still brunet even at her age fully bushy pussy lips.

Hey babe, he smuthered peg with his customer I'm home hug and liplock. I am pretty sure it is called "x and o". Every time he entered their home he always remind her that in is life his ultimately need his fulfilled when she entered into his eyesight.

Hell of a day? She asked. She loved the X's and O's and the rest of what comes along the way toy but she knew him better than he knew himself. Yeah squad raided a porno being made. The wives natural eye peeking came from the side of her profile. Her left eyelid that unh, unh slightly more closed than the right one. She a good deal shorted then he so the upward angle lender to the catechism of her expression. She even knew his broadness was looking the other direction, his back fully turned towards her when she gave it. He had to view the tape, cautioning himself to show her her respect by using the word video, Lo and behold Miss Brenda Karen was one of the main attractions, here he was hoping to engage a videoier night by using the word attractions, rather than participants.

Down on the table with a palm protecting and silent force went his soup spoon the Governor's daughter? Naturally using her enlightened and totally caught off guard, yet believing to the hilt voice. Yeeup. His hands washed he pecked peg on vaginal area his left arm wrapped around her buttocks as he sat down to dinner.

Dinner was great. He had three full helpings. Each covered the full of his ten and half inch Pfoltagraff Seraphina Blue Stoneware dinner plate.

He actually wanted buy the Richard Ginor Oriente Italian- Malachite. He liked the stand out blue and green color and it's name.

Pegantha held out on it. She held solemnly and quietly held to herself. Good you like that. They will become my second set. Your anniversary present. That glorifying feminist inner smile had her all a glow.

Their second go round came a mere six or maybe seven minutes after their first, the sheets on both their lower legs.

She in the middle of having the onset of another well earned orgasm lied flat on her back, leg flat on the sheet knees locked, calves muscles tight, thighs muscle hardening, big toes angled towards his ankles between her legs three touching toes of each foot curled like knots and both little toes on their way to catching up with their three bigger sisters.

His thickness has not let her hole in the least bit. It has been completely imbedded and giving only the necessary inward pump one inside of her as to lift her labia minor a upwards exposing the fullness of her clit. The side wards motions had already began both of their desired culminations his balls in the their big sack lie directly on the moistened sheets. Blesset has crawled from the linolean floor up the blanket and sheet and has with the stealth of he felineness positioned herself in the only spot and had been licking his ball sack for the last couple of minutes. No teeth, only lips and sardined pussy juiced smelling tongue.

The detective Sergeant's flat ass tightened to tone of the phrase hard as a rock. The telephone rang. It was his line specifically for his employment.

He pressed radial twenty seven minutes later. Hello this Sera Elizabeth Johnston. We need you at the Chief's office a.s.a.p. it was the chief of police's personal adjutant. She too usually worked daylight hours only. He headed back to work. Pegantha and Blessit in turn went back to pleasuring one another. Each of their tongues lightly, sensually caressing.

CHAPTER THREE

COVER UP

Each of the nine officers that worked inside the precinct that night three days ago had been interviewed and signed the deal made to them by Alphonso Capers, district attorney.

To keep the general public from being informed of the mass rape of one Ms. Karen Brenda who also knew and agreed to the city and state deal.

She would receive settlement of two million dollars for each member of the vice squad who had molested her while incarcerated. Non disclosure agreement was signed in order of her to receive major parts in every movie the state would have filmed for the next ten years.

Nine former officers did four years behind bars in a state facility. Their charges would be dereliction of duty it was arranged so their confessions would not interfere with any other police case, covering the city, should they however violate the nondisclosure agreement full charges would be brought along with contact violation and thirty years inside federal penitentiary would be the least time they would serve. If one broke their word, then all would face that same penalty.

The acceptance by all parties weather they knew it or not kept the knowledge of the governor's being an animal fucker from being exposed.

First class lieutenant detective Martin also liked the deal he had gotten. Pegantha was so proud of him. She ate out his asshole slowly with many tongue flicking French kisses that her respect for him had been unnecessarily reinforced. Blessit had a few extra sardines to gorge on, half a one at a time slowly was muscle puckered from Pegantha's anus hole while on her knees at the foot of the bed.

The final part of the deal went to the D.A. capers would be replacing the present deputy mayor on the next election which posed a shoe in for re-election.

CHAPTER FOUR

DIRECTIVES

So what do you think questioned the idea promoter. Seems it would make a good movie J.B. Blane answers. Okay! So what are the buts to your comment inquires the idea guy. No buts. Can you not understand when I say I like it goes the largest porn movie backer in the last twenty years. All I see that could be in the way is if you get greedy.

Two mil, no, but how about we say seven hundred fifty thou and two point four percent of the profit. An inward smile of triumph. Deal. Missy print it out. Miss missy Chen, J.B's personal secretary opens her brief case brings out the mini computer and printer. Three minutes later papers are handed out signed and a copy to each.

The cash goes your account at the Republic bank in your savings account. Says Chen.

He calls his bank and tells them he is on his way to withdraw ten thousand dollars. The money is there. He knew it would be. Let's commemorate comes the joyous J.B. we will take my car to your bank and bring back here so you pick-up yours.

In the Rolls Phanton eight Champagne is passed. Cocaine is offered. The ideaman refuses the coke but takes hefty slugs of the sparkley.

Chen after taking a small cocaine snort in both her little Phillipean nostrils gets to her job J.B. has a massive, and I do mean missive sized cock. Chen could not possibly get half the breadth of the almost grapefruit sized thickness, but her tongue was working miracles in the spectators mind.

Bet her asshole can hold two kickland golf balls muses J.B. her panties are now removed and her asshole shows multiple tears, most unhealed. J.B. has been busy.

They ride around until J.B. cums surprisingly he has very little semen.

They arrive at the bank. A few minutes later ten thousand dollars are in the ideaman's front trouser pocket. He gets in the Rolls.

Chen starts on his rather small dick. As she does J.B. instructs the driver to take them back to when the car was left.

The ideaman's eyes close. He is fast asleep. The chanpaign was dosed. J.B. rolls him on his stomach and rams his now fully thirteen inch long dick in the ideaman's ass and fucks him for over an hour. His asshole has been ripped to shreds.

Take me to a department store orders J.B. to the driver as he tears the once kinda tight anus of the ideaman.

Coming out of the department store, Chen phones the driver. The Rolls pulls up as she exits the two glass does and gets in the car.

They retrouser the ideaman but with a new pair of underwear in place of the ones that had been blood stains from the flow that fell on them white on the floor out of the ideaman's not soon to heal ass.

Back to his car, J.B. puts the ideaman under the steering wheel of the six year of Cadillac, locks the car door, returns to his new Phantom eight and drives on.

Back at the hotel the two exit the car. First J.B. Blanc, but befoss Missy Chen takes her exit, she removes the Phantom's V.A. disc.

In the suite while J.B. showers, Chen edits the taping of the rape in the Bolls's back seat. Putting in a tital in the front of the recording. It is titled Barak O. Obama's, Porn Deal is sealed.

Obama awakes in his used Cadillac. He sees the note left him by J.B. it has these words. The price of dealing with me. It is hand signed, James Buchanan Blanc.

As he thinks the champaign must have overwhelmed him, he remembers the Chen dick sucking and a slight alarm comes as he checks his front pocket. That alarm goes away to a greater realization of life, even before he feels the lump of folded one hundred dollar bills. The pain in his ass causes him more than a wince. He cries out in anguish. Then he fools the wetness where he is sitting. The pain persists and would persist for months to comes.

CHAPTER FIVE

AS THE WORLD TURNS

You better not go to sick call. The bleached blondes walked out of the cell. It is free time so unless an inmate requests her cell door locked all the doors remained open.

Then went to the common area. They gave the world all is clear. That they had finished with the prisoner in cell B-102. The word did not really need to be given, as the other inmates saw them leave and those who had paid notice of their leaving did see them in the common area near the south side television area where the game table that eat times of light lockdown were used for breakfast, lunch or dinner. Intermingling but all of them smelled of the odor of freshly having sex with another female who had not wash. Damn I stink said one, silent agreement. We need to let that pig wash her ass. Hmmphs came from a couple. The others just a light weight glare. That's a no. two took showers.

One, sat at card table smelling her fingers.

The cell in B-110 has been dealing cocaine powder for the last year without any impunity. The drug is brought into prison by correctional office Lynne Abraham. She is assigned to the Culinary Area. Usually a quarter ounce per week. Favors are done for her. Some of the other C.O's. know of the drug trafficking so favors are done for them to keep the operation running smoothly. It has been hoped that B-102 would catch on and show a little spunk. In order to stop her forceful rapes from occurring but to this date she has not caught one to who is in the operation.

It has been too long. So orders are sent into the prison through C.O. Abrahams to get it over with anyway and get it over with soon.

Kept off the television airways yet flooded with newspapers and radio news stations former vice police officer convicted of gross dereliction of duty commits suicide in cell by hanging. Television may have alerted the other nine.

One week later the story could not be smothered. It was planned that way. Various peoples problems were solved all in one stroke. The banners read twenty seven dead in prison riot- attempted escape. Over the next couple of days all the names were given to public communications conveyances. In those names listed alphabetically were Johan Hex and Lidia Kit Chen. A short foot note was added to small town newspapers that those two at one time had served as police officers on the vice squad. The part that was with held was that the two corpses once served together and were punitively release with seven other such officers. Nor was it released until the next day that a third of those officers had hung herself in her cell in another penal institution just one week earlier.

Hewlitte Redmond was moving slowly, slow enough to satisfy the governor and his daughter. Caution is paramount Redmond's mind locked. Three down, six to go.

Peter Benkman, a country and state prison coroner had done the wrong thing in having a massive drinking problem. He soon was shown a video of his wife in a compromising position with other man. A three way. He was then shown two single photos of those two men bound hand and foot spread eagled, naded and bamber smeared over the entirety of their bodies. Hogs were eating there dead bodies. Two bullet holes in each of their heads. Benkman noted his watch date was may 05, 1986 8:07 AM.

The autopsy was forged in the corners gratitude for hiding, no not hiding but rather neglecting to note the evidence of the second and third former vice cops repeated anal ravishings.

The second corner only took three thousand cash dollars.

Mey Westford who was corporal and superviser in the precinct the date Brenda Karen's revenge is being taken for found herself with fourth stage rectal cancer that had spread rapidly throughout her body. The cancer as cancer off times does had spread to her abdomen, missed her left long but not her right one and had terminate the woman when it encompassed the whole of her heart. No medicine on Earth could have halted her demise. The prison hospital oncologist two weeks earlier won his auto claim of six hundred nine thousand dollars and four cents.

Needless to say the autopsy did not make any notation of massive rectal tearing. Nor was written of her throat and her esophagus had major remarkable irritations. Small spinters of wood were found in both areas.

Four.

Number five came about shortly thereafter. Butter Bean, real name Emma Samms was the head dike in this prison. No crime came about without same kickback to her. When a crime did happen her hand hold on the inmates was so tight that you had better not complain, not even to her. This was because before any crime small too large took you needed her approval.

Melba Monroe found this out fast when she started her four years sentence for gross dereliction of duty. She put all of her commicery money on Butter Bean's books. Books is were you put money to spend in prison. You want shoes the cost comes off of your books.

When Melba More came in she made Butter Bean forty thousand dollars richer. A fortune is prison. She also lent he tongue out to Butter Bean for whatever. Butter Bean chose it to be used four.

Melba was summoned to Butter Beans cell. On her way there she tripped over her own feet and fell three tiers down to a steal reinforced cement floor to her death.

Butter Bean had just insured her continuing rule over this prison. If such a thing would not have accidentally happened then a transfer to another such prison awaited in the Deputy Wardens office.

Five gone. Six, Seven Eight and nine have been arranged.

One last meeting took place.

A week later the decision arrived via private corporate jet.

The pilot called back to the executive bedroom one of the floozies the execs flew in from Beirut.

Eyes meeting. He smirks. The Floozie glowers but strips. The pilot drops his trousers and drops to his knees as he the tiny creamy tits with ripples protruding from them about and an inch or so. Off comes the plaid skirt and panties both together hitting the floor. He sucks the she males long thick dick. In moments it is too is protruding in the same manner as the nipples.

The pilot's mouth goes almost all its length but his tongue flicks towards the dangling hairy balls to no avail.

Floozie holds the back of his head. He somewhat holds back still slurping. Back to his neck goes the cock. He is held there. He gets used to it hitting his tonsil and sucks on. This time minutes later that nut sock is acquired.

Floozie comes. He still sucks. Floozie pisses a stream until only drops can come out. He sucks on. Licks, kisses goes upwards to the tip not yet caring to release the whole of it. The floozie pulls the meaty stick out and slaps the co-pilot in the face with the wet dick, raises it up and gives way to the bottom of the balls sack. A tongue flicks the asshole's pathway. Then the round buttocks are parted and a tongue goes inside the hole whap! Goes the dick down on the co-pilots nose.

An about face is I have to say done with a graceful turn as the she-he bends over and each of the floozie's separates it's side checks and the ass kissing, fingering, licking goes on along with a wet tongue licking the asscrack up to the bottom of the spine as the tongue on it's way down passes the hole to lick that gaggling ballsack a solid and loud gift explodes in both nostrils.

That solid fired is soft and adhere to: his face from: under his eyes: on and in the nose: on both lip: his chin and had a couple of flecks on his neck.

She-he turned around busting a nut while inserting that dick again to the back of the neck pushing the solid waste in common terms called shit through the mouth and introducing it to the esophogelia cilia.

Some of the shit left the nostril the co-pilot still wanted to breath and with the condition his mouth was in the nose blowing was his only choice.

Done for this time the floozie walks to a purse, takes out a nine millimeter, shows it is loaded and begins to get the clothing on again. As the she mate leaves the jet these words are spoken. I know you don't expect me to sock or fuck that tiny dick of yours, then left.

CHAPTER SIX

AVIAN FLU

The end of the game was afoot. The last four were sentenced to spending their four years in the same prison.

The world was alerted not to come to visit any of their family serving time in the prison. The prison guards had temporary shanty housing erected on the facilities grounds. They were not allowed to leave. Avian flew had struck.

Twenty two hundred in matter were sentenced to long terms. Three hundred to less than thirty years. Two hundred guards and other employees where there. Thirty four hundred in all were quarantined in all. The four sparrows that had gotten inside were all dead. Three to the surgeons table were sacrificed and the last had died of the flew that is the one that caused it all. A tailor maid epidemic. One of the three dissected had a curious case of bird syphillus.

Coughing and wheezing sounds were as prevalent in that facility. More so than the mandatory vaccines and personal distributing the doses of Peramavir. The introvenus doses were given to most of the population. Some inmates eighty six in all and guards totally three died.

That concluded the six, seventh eighth and last targets

The coroner somehow got to examine the particular four was a Doctor Luellen vest.

She became overwhelmed with grief and stopped examining the women's cases. Her reasoning, too many of her kind in imprisonment.

She wiped away more than a single tear when doing her highly successful novel my sisters. Why? A book on criminal life persued rather than a safe and secure home through the art of education and sucking up to legality.

The Li, Scorcaiz movie was a rave at the box offices and a sequel was being highly touted for it's demand by those who paid to see it.

Four months post.

I want to introduce to you at my great pleasure a fine man, an outstanding American, my friend and running mate for the office of vice president of these here United States of America and former governor of Washington D.C.

CHAPTER SEVEN

HER FINALLY

Two days ago

She entered, had coffee.

You came. Uh huh. Gents our star. The last film is beginning in Russia, China, Poland Brazil and few other places. Over ten million orders. This script is better. She began by unzipping his denim cargo pants. Shocked by the pink and red flesh that fell to her hand and face, she wanted to understand, so she looked upwards. She had only started to bob down and what she saw forced her withdrawal. At first her mind did not want to believe, that what she saw was factitious, then as the producers body began to limply descend to the carpet her head turned. A natural reaction and what further viewed coldly firmly established she needed to go. Escape in hurry! Came her inner self's pontification.

Staying low, a crouching haste she unlatched the door and ran like a bat out of hell. She did not take the time to close the door.

He walked out of the warehouse Brenda had just escaped, closed the door and pulled the portcullis to the ground and without any indication that he had murdered the six peoples left behind laggardly pereganated around the corner to his new model customized white Coruette Stingray.

Brenda arrived at the secured parking lot. When BMW was brought to her by Bernie, the name on the attendants shirt tag, she got in and saw the piece remnant of forehead skin on her own brow in the vanity mirror. She brought herself from the momentary memory, wipe it away to the passenger seat and processed the thought. Go home came her bosom subconscious inner articulate. On her way home a bit more than a few drops of the pouring rain got her arm wet. She gave it a good try to withstand the malodorous expurgations, but those jalapeno tacos results...

Brenda, Brenda, shouted the voice. The shouter got on her Xpro one fifty and followed Brenda to her flat. As Brenda pulled to her apartment building, Elise Iapp pulled up to her driver's side window. Even in the downpour the BMW's window was lowered fully into the car down. El what are you doing in this rain asked Brenda. Need you girl. Can I come up or are you about to get busy up there? Now come on in. I'll get the doorman to get a guess parking pass and send it up. Get out that rain.

The two caught the elevator.

Naked as jaybirds they went into the laboratory, Elise got into the shower first. Brenda apprehended towels and robes and hung them up on marble hooks.

Once the street dirt was elimated, the towels in the white items hamper and mini robes adorned bet not fastened. The feeling of loose breast and uncovered patches of sculptured vulva hair looked delightful and the freedom...

Elise entertained herself with a lemon wedge from the refrigerator. Brenda held the strawberry brandy ice cube by its popsicle stick holder. The two were raised in their respective homes by affluent biological parent. They had cloth napkins in their other hand. They were not carrying themselves like uncivilized hogs.

Brenda said to Elise, how are classes?, insinuating about one student Elise was but was not supposed to be sleeping with. I am still employed. No one had found out of the situation. None that would bring it to the university's board anyway.

Some music? KATT. So on went KATT country western.

Homemade cheeseburgers micro-waved came soon. While eating Brenda asked El what do need Boobala? I'll get to that but you seemed a little elsewhere when you said come on up. Is everything ok? No. things have gotten gross lately. You mean since your pops got to run for VP? That is not it. The I'll instead of I will, was noted mentally, so Brenda asked Elise why the vernacular change? That I'll instead of I will. Where did that come from students are wearing me down I guess. Her head kind of titled the righted quickly. Those tits did something they not often do, they jiggled. Elise has thirty eight cis, but they pressed straight out from her ribs. No falling downward there. Not even a slight say and they were tight and firm, so they hardly every giggled.

Brenda Karen has a stacked defecation style body, but her thirty six's fell downward when unbraed. They jiggled even in iron like supporter. She envied those and inwardly wished an optical illusion was with her every time Elise was topless.

The desk rings in on her apartment plane. Ms. Karen. A mister Leblanc from the Armory is downstairs. He mentions an appointment ma'am. Yes, I know of him. Direct him straight away please? Yes Miss Karen. And thank you Elise ask Brenda, should I leave? Nor sug. He is an aims dealer. I am having a garter pistol Taylor forged. He will only be a couple minutes and then, if you do not mind we can get to why you flagged me down.

Brenda you were so-you. Rubbing your juicy on that gun salesman hand every time he had to take a measurement on your thighs. He did not complain. Did he? No, and he was so damned handsome. He had to be wearing boxers, briefs would not hold something so long in place. I think he licked his fingers when he went out door. You hussy. Have you fucked him yet?

That is how he got the appointment. Big dick. Last a long time. Poor as hell though.

Aha! Goes Elsie, the fund raiser for that guy. This is why I flagged you over. Here is check. Their fingertips touch, hold position, caress. They are on the double ottoman tongues and fingers going in and out of themselves and each other. Brenda though was does disrupt her fullness of sexual attributions. Only because Elsie loves the affection of that as a finishing touch, giving and receiving it anterior to her exiting whether going home, to the family, a social function or any of the multitudinous segues in her lifestyle.

Before the two allowed themselves a time honored tradition allotted designation sleep valued acceptances of one another intermingled and took what seemed allotted cadances of chances and rehearsed sexual perfectionisms.

In the morning Brenda ran her tongue the up, down and around the prior nights neglected at first flaccid and then erecting and finally to a full erected nine inch penis. This morning the vulva it had at first lingered seemingly lifeless but like the mummy of hold made to achieve it's pole-like status is now being neglected. Yes Elise is a transformer, one pussy, one ass, a hidden set of testicles and a dick in size length and thickness used properly would surely consume the passion of most feminine. Elise was a professional in the department of phallusing a cont.

Just before that morning Elise halter in the apartment front door away turned towards Brenda and asked Brenda. Brenda what did the recently divorced man on the toilet who had been constituted must of the think about as he finally expelled saying that's a load off my mind? Brenda never did get the solutions to El's quips unless told, so she said nothing. He was thinking at the divorce he gave his wife one final, I was thinking we should reunite. His ex-wife said to him you were thinking like an ass.

While waiting for her motor scooter she gathered together portions of seven years ago. Before the operation. When she ached to not only consider what it felt like to a man to run up inside of a woman, to get his dick sucked and fuck the shit out of her only to put the fecal clump he pulled out of her hole and put it while still on the head of his dick in her mouth along with his dick and have her suck his dick. How a man felt while getting head to piss in her mouth and know she swallows of his piss and then genuinely sweetly sucks his dick. Elise remembered she was a four times over deca-millionaire, so she got a dick and with had balls put inside her. As she had done with Brenda Karen last night.

She was then seven years ago a manmade hermaphrodite. And she solemnly, though with stealth ask from her heart and mind. Forgive me god, if I did sinfully.

CHAPTER EIGHT

MOM

A pain ran through my him. Darn it I in advertantly rolled over on my right side. Was my subconscious aware I was doing that. Darn I think it was. Almost sure I remember thinking of it just as I was turning. Perhaps a strong warning. I was in the process of making my body follow my minds full awareness and attempting to not care about my own comfort. At least or a little more so I did not fully torn onto my him yes, a warning. Back on my back. I tell my body. My mind fully conscious. Hey do not forget to say please. It was not a request. It was an order. Okay than thank you. Good going. Never forget your manners or Misses Leona D just might come down from heaven and kick you in the shin. You remember her. The woman God put on loan to you to give you birth. The one who did you right. She stood by your side almost always. You do remember her, the one who introduced you to God whose name in the "The holy Bible" at least in one versions, is jealous. The one who had you accept Christ as your lord and savior.

No need to wake up.

CHAPTER NINE

We Tory on this country on this little blue marble Earth call ourselves Americans. And we have the absolute right to do so, let the three hundred sixty million of us be not forgetful of our neighbors to the north. Canadians all. Also have the absolute right to call themselves Americans as do we. Also our neighbors to the south. They are various in nations unlike our neighbors to the north, also have the absolute right to call themselves Americans. Let all of us Tory stand together in one accord. Let us all request that the leaders of this nation together with the many leaders of those nations join together to protect the sovereign borders of all Americans.

The new vice-president elect left that podium and only two of the billions of people he averted to knew that the basic concept of a western hemisphere pulling together as one came from an author of a series of books each entitled, even shorter stories.

The thunderous applause roared from that day.

One may impishly inquire where was said author at the during the moments his idea was ceremoniously usurped. He had not obtained monetary riches at that time and was existing in a furnished rented room with an accompanying private bath for his own personal use writing a pornographic novel that could easily be turned into a theatre screening as was. The devil in Miss Jones. Porn with a good story that came from a book whereas even a Christian church had little bias. Truthful, disgusting, sinful and mournful sells by the millions. Other than conundrum, he lingered his Sherlock Holmes-ess brain on the blockage of chuck Verrill answering pursuit of a literary agent. If this were a computer problem, than where is and how to access the back door without getting enslaved by the legal system and also not being physically assaulted might be nice.

You do understand by physically assaulted I meant hurt.

Geez how many people are going to find out what Tory means now that the VP referred to us as Tory?

That was really what she was thinking as she watched the speech on the news update.

At least she did not call the bro out by thinking aloud so people who were not presently eating out her pussy could comprehend that her time is being wasted. His tongue and method had been boring her for over a half hour. Her next thought he has good teeth and his breath is fresh, so at least I am getting my pussy hole cleaner.

Been here a good minute. I give him until the time. I finish counting all the little white different shaped unicorns. Hey they are all white. A couple of then do have gold colored pointy horns on there foreheads, could they all be white because of that Miriam Webster thing. Unicorns and white both pure truthful and good. Oh well, fifty six of them. I got to go home dude. Hunh. The son of a bitch! She thought. Its time. I have to get in. Maybe we can hook up later. That is what she said, but what she meant is that phrase, don't call me. I'll call you. Which means beat it bub.

Dressed and exiting into the hallway. Peeu. Those expergations I did in there are really lingering in this hallway must be clinging to his hairs too. Let's add them up. Mustache beard: nose: eyelashes: scalp: pectorals: underarms: stomach: and legs. She consciously left out his pubic area. His prefer uh not that mentionable get in her VW and got out of Dodge, only to return if in the houses and arms of his neighbors.

I try to weakly, meekly force myself into hypnagogia, but my mind tells me, oh no you do not! You have been in this place a couple of times. You are not going to wake up and walk as a protest. Stay asleep. Hey! That voice that was in my head, it wasn't even time. It is a woman's. Slumber abated all cerebration.

CHAPTER TEN

FAMILY TIES

The secretaries sat there trying not to directly ask. Everything was straight forward with these old friends despite the truths each knew of the others bosses.

There is something different about bosses and their secretaries in politics verses bosses and their secretaries in industry.

The bosses wives in politics rarely if ever are put in a position to say to her husband's lap. In industry, well I am sure you have heard the talk.

Okay so interns in politics do no follow the secretary theory. Yes, theory.

Odd it would be to have a, let us make use of the office of the Senate, to have a Senator's private secretary enter the room while a Senator's own wife in going down on him and the huffy secretary yells to the wife get your filthy ass mouth off my man! Some female Senators secretary enters the room and the senator's husband is having a hairy or a shaved pussy nosh and the secretary gives a yawp get my man's mouth away from your dirty cunt, you cunt!

Mayhap that is why in politics Secretary's day is still an endearing day to spouses of the politicians. Interns have no day. Yes. You may have theorized that the ladies are celebrating their day.

The particular one of high wishes to end the other incognizance is Billondria O'daily the senior most is years and political experience who last night had a date after forty one months of inactivity. She was asked out by a peer of her age group, Benjamin Lopell, a owner of nine taverns and two bowling alleys all quite lucrative businesses and a widower of two years after thirteen years in a second but good marriage.

O'Daily never used illegal narcotics was staunchly against them as was her boss. She knew what all the others were hoping happened and would not ask in order not to jinx their dreams.

O'Daily gave them one proper clue. The only one they would need to oypher it all out. She said to them, a little pot never hurt anyone.

Size and position.

The gaiety for the women became enormously elated and long lasting, well past the own holiday.

O'Daily was the secretary to the president's personal aid.

The tavern is crowded. It is crowded every day most of the served customers take two of doubles. Those drinks average fifteen a glass a piece. This is one of the waterholes owned by Lopell. Lopell is a alcoholic. He stopped going down crazy road when he was seventeen years old and never took the time to even look backwards.

Betty Chegault was next in order of whose boss carried the bigger stick in DC Chegault although working in the white house was third secretary to the newly elected vice president was about to be richer than eighty percent of the elitist of political figures. Her husband Yues saint Pruit Chegault is partner with Blen Deist, the coinventors of preferred denture top. Their top allow the wearers to tastes more of the flavors from food while eating A simple elegant solution changed in two ways from the formerly popular, most sought and becoming rapidly the most acquired prosthethis. The top prosthetic matched the bottom in design. Formerly top of the denture covered a large part of the roof of the wearers mouth therefore blocking food from contacting that area. Many taste buds are located in the roof of the mouth. With the top only covering a half inch of the top gum all the taste buds are now exposed to the food the wearer consumed. The only drawback and this we keep to ourselves is the newly wed wife, loved enormously by her husband, but she did not possess the cunning culinary skill. Hee hee hee.

Betty is a fan of double oh seven. She must be. Her drink of choice. Vodka Martini, shaken not stirred. Double.

She is also a total fitness freak. Not for herself she shows love for woman kind by owning three hundred female only fitness spas in seven countries in the western hemisphere. She owns exactly zero in the eastern hemisphere. She plans to franchise none.

Xzi Mit Zao is married to an autor in Japanese Karate movie. He has been nominated for best supporting actor in the only American made movie he has ever been. Xzi Mit Zao is the younger sister to the president.

Xzi drinks only saki hot. Never does she have more than one. Never does she double her drink up Xzi also is a certified super genius with an sq. of one hundred ninety one. Xzi is senior secretary to Hip Pao Hu, the most wealthy Japanese arms agent to live to date. Xzi, though she is unaware at the present and will learn of it until two months from a day ago is one month pregnate. She will give birth to nine very healthy Akachan, making all her family Kyokutan'na Hokri ni omou.

CHAPTER ELEVEN

Word got quickly two things must happen. The first thing some put at second most paramount. Thinking about the importance order some concurred some did not concur. Both however if not adhered to would not could, but will cruse severe, writer, producer, director and whoever else penalties. Keep it unknown and no more Brenda Karen skin flicks. Both were accepted on penalty of death should both or even one not be.

Robert Allen's funeral director to the stars got the dead bodies, prepared all of them for their families. In each of their forty thousand dollar proceedings the bodies looked as though they would wake as soon as the cycle of sleep had it's temporary demise.

The mortician did excellent work. Artistic work. He receive for his cunning excellent artistic pay from each of the families burying their departed father, husband, dad, son or granddad. Whichever fir. Unbeknownst to the families he earned more financial capital from the underground body parts mafia than for the legal proceedings, the last now ending. He was an excellent salesman.

Should proceedings had gone away his two piece holster on the lower back behind his loose fitting professionals jacket holds in each of the twin holster pockets is a fifty caliber fifty AE. Desert Eagle. In his get-away vehicle should a possible unlucky customer follow him in his white Ford Bronco is a Big Babalon, secured and hidden in the rear seating wired to target and fire from his steering wheel, if necessary even while he was manipulating his way through traffic.

One man attended each and every one of those funerals. Seeing if there was a visitor or were visitors who came to all of the funerals and or all of the viewing. One detective Martin.

CHAPTER TWELVE

This is one of those types of books that end without the full story completely wound-up. When I came out of my sleeping period and became fully aware, I remembered not one spec of an iota of what the chimera did reveal. Guess I will never be the bearer who does the endowing of that vision to you. I am so, so sorry. Please forgive me.

The end

BONUS STORY

WHAT GLASS CEILING?

CHAPTER ONE

In the inner workings of this planet Earth something major has gone awry. God found that out the hard way.

People believed those that did believe thought that God was perfect. That he could not make a mistake, but that has been proven incorrect.

You can ask why me a full Christian, one who totally believes in God's existence could bring himself to put such a thing, a byte of infortion as the above in print.

Take as gospel, I did, and I am not the first one which explains without a doubt that I am not the only one.

Should I even again as prior to this time and together inclusive with this time write on God I write what I can prove to be so.

Where do I hide such proof? It is not a hidden fact but in the everyday plain sight of the Holy Bible, and what is written within its covers.

If anyone and I write including God does something on purpose and then verbally admits to all the masses after he has done it complains that it grieved him, than I must say even I myself had done something and wish I had not, a mistake was made.

God created man and woman. It was done on one of the six days of creation before he took a rest on the seventh, Sabbath, day.

God found that man was... so, he made it rain forty days and forty nights.

Please God in all the sins done by myself and my direct blood line, please forgive us? Thank you.

The thank you art, I was thought by the woman you loaned to me to bring me to you. She did. Thank you from us all!!

CHAPTER TWO

Y ou see that sixty eight year old very, very handsome old guy sitting on those steps on the Vandelorian Majestic Suites building there. He is a great man. So you may come up with adversity to me describing him as being great. Solely because there are some fifty heavy duty trash bags sitting on the rear paved way to the suites.

He is there by his choice. His own volition. He had been there for all of twelve minutes awaiting the RINO a private company contracted vehicle to the whole of the cities most influential business and skyscraper rentals.

RINO is Mafia owned and operated. It is part of the mob's dual decoded protection rocket.

No better place for his reasoning for waiting on the spot. The kenetics of his brain allotted this area to be perfect. His thoughts and his thoughts only.

There were no cameras in this alleyway. He did not drink. Nor did he smoke. His hands had on each two rubber surgery gloves. No possible way to alert any of his being there, no DNA would be left when he left.

His class would allow him no eating and or drinking there. His cleanliness of personality kept him from urinating, even in a bottle he could cap, nor a coffee cup with a lid. Defecating too was not a vehicle he had succumbed to.

His only clue that he had been there is his singing of the new national anthem for the United States, Written by Country western super superstar Toby Keith, Courtesy of the Red, White and Blue, yet none heard him as this one was one time he quieted his voice on the lyrics of his favorite rendition.

The old national anthem sucks nard. The ending of a thought had occurred as the diesel of the RINO engine came into his ears.

The truck got to the mound of refuse and he picked up a full hefty bag then tossed it into a cavernous waste recepicle. He then helped put in the rest of the trash, waved the guys and the thickly built Puerto Rican female off as the truck rambled on to its next destination.

I guess not he had thought of his musing earlier weather married women on a beach during the hotness of summer in their thong bikinis wear their wedding rings should their husbands not be present.

He felt just the slightest bit empty as he made his left turn on departure from the alley. No answer had come to him.

Although there was an overcast brought out the sun glasses.

His plan was so well thought he noticed what seemed to be a homeless man sitting on a double high milk crate seat with of all things a shoe shine kit, but passed up the chance. No need to push it.

On his merry way he went. Satisfied his crime will never be uncovered.

She was on the Seattle Washington Downtown Circulation bus. There were a couple of cons doing a three card Monte hustle. She did not need the money but decided to break them anyway. Send them back to wherever they came from.

She stood along side of the gamer and the cards as she had been taught. I have three hundred dollars she said. Can I play? She asked. Show the color of your money the card handler said. She brought out a one hundred dollar bill. Sat it on the makeshift corrugated board.

The card handler started shifting the three cards showing a queen and two jacks. One red and one black.

Where is your money she asked of him? He brought out a folded wad and placed two fifty's beside her Franklin. Before we go on she softly said, where I come from you guys give odds. You're supposed to be the one with fast hands, so no problem. Two too one he said. No she replied three to one.

His game was to alleviate her that cash so he boldly put up three hundred. She toughed the left card to her and won. He felt like an ass.

Give you a shot at losing the rest of your wad she said. The bait is set.

I have four hundred. You want to cover it. One of his backmen watched a little closer while at attempting to be only slightly interested. That is how she found which of the twenty or so passengers he was. She was still watchful. There may be a third.

He again brought out his was. Two too one he said. She replied no, she put three hundred of the four in her pocket. You want your money. It's going to cost you to try and get it back. One C-note at a time. Fine he said. Putting up two hundred. No way. Five to one. Then she put the full four hundred on the corrugated. I can't cover the whole two g's he said.

Ok what you can. He put up six hundred dollars. She took back two hundred. Three too one she said. Deal he said. No backing away was a three card Monte player trait and she knew.

She picked up the eight hundred dollars after she chose the red queen without a doubt.

The stir on the bus ended in a minute. She sat down in the bus's last row of seats.

She had again as since the first day of moving into a Seattle a year ago told mental note of the public transits bus's cleanliness. Not like filthydelphia she again came to the realization that people here were better than those in Pennsylvania where she was born and raised.

Sadness hit her to remember that place but the joy of her surroundings kicked that feeling to the curb. Not a clean curb like the ones where she now abided, but a trash, needle and empty drug container covered sidewalks like the ones she moved away from.

She stayed alert and rode the bus to the end of the line where the three of the Monte card crew got off.

Her inner smile glowed all over her. She stayed on and rode the same transit back to her actual stop. Since they did get back on, figuring she must have been wise that they might have robbed her to get back there lost ungains, so she released her three eighty from he hand in her jacket pocket.

She would not be the hero on this day.

Laura Bettison, the transit driver also seemed to show some relief. She had watched.

CHAPTER THREE

Her complete nakedness showing she reached for one of the smaller hot pink towels dampening her wet from the shower hair. Picks up another from next to the wicker hamper where the first one was tossed and makes hat of it. Then she dries her pubs with the wash cloth. Discards it into the same hamper. As she adjust the full body towel around he once naked and still dripping water body she again pays attention to her wrap around sound coming from the super hero movie she has on her living room projected screen the sound happens still. She knows nearly every line and yet there are sounds.

The actors voices. Talking to each other. Holding conversations not on tapes that were recorded when the movie was first filmed. The conversations do two things. They both progress from the last viewing carrying on their talks with the left off one when the projector was turned off and also new ones occur current events of the historical happenings of today.

The one thing that clouds her mind in why do the talks go on from where they had left off before. Why do they not converse with each other while the movie was turned off and she had slept or cavorted outside. One other thing began to totally worry her. On occasion they characters in the movie reminded her of her own thoughts she had had on a scene when that scene was again played as though she was being included. She began to test it. She commented to the movies characters on the comments made to her. They in turn were not discourteous. They replied.

This better be a tall drink of water or I am subject to hang up the phone. Those were the words that sub-angrily told her the phone was ringing. It was personalized ring tone. She changed her ring tone almost every day. She was one who became bored very posthaste and basically hell-for-leather and no apologia necessary.

She often used many synonyms for her quickness of being bored in conversation. The only one she purposely chose to neglect was lickity-split phrase, deciding that would never bring on her lackadaisical trait.

Hi auntie Em, call Celeesze's small mezzo soprano love call. Cel, as her aunt called her was nine years old. An appraised, tested and certified genious and a future, near future sure to an operatic superstar. Cel's favorite musical instrument though did not fit her future in musical expertise, which by the way she had mastered to perfection was the Bass guitar, which also somehow did not fit her lead voice when singing her favored country western music.

You coming? Went the musical inquisition. Mom says you are. Dad said you are, and you said you are.

Can I get a phrase or a word or two in edgewise my little love one? Cel gives silent. Naturally I'll be there, Joyousness on the other end of the phones sound waves. Can I bring something for you? Just you auntie. Love you. Dad's giving me the say help for him sign. An command he's giving me that we going to be tardy.

Some people are crazy. Or they just psychic? Going on his way to the front door Dion waves to his sister on the other end of the phone, as if she could see him making the gesture, he was socially satisfied and Celeesze's catches up to him in the door, her video game on Candy Crush.

George Blessing and extra-ordinarily attractive wife Grenda Eliz live next door to Em. George has come from the elevator heading to his door. Em gets a feeling, cracks her front door and George Blessing is passing her apartment door. She opens the door something startling him. He sees the body towel and holds his impression. Em with a beckoning forefinger halts him. He a total gentleman since they met each other eleven years ago at this very same spot, steps to her while hoping none are in her apartment demanding a violent attention.

Em, when he is a few inches from her face drops the towel, Em braces and sexually French kisses him. Deep tongued. He does pull back but it takes a few moments. One of two of those moments are due to his being surprised.

Em smile. Eyes glistening. Re-enters her apartment. The door she tries slowly to close. The towel is in the way of the door frame.

George happy, but in his state he still remembered Grenda, his Grenda and what she has waiting twenty yards and seconds away. He chose Eliz and went home.

The towel is retrieved. The door is closed. That I'll touch that hot bi---. He will fu__ you soon. He will also be thinking of me. Enjoy.

A quarter of an hour later the batteries in her vibrating double was put to rest in the pocket of the plush velvet four cushioned sofa.

The cushions were barely spotted but had a paucity of dampness. Em would never admit it. Not even to herself but sometime after Grenda's husband passed her mind she had to force out the vision of three men having their way with her. Leaving her insides and cheek bones around her mandibular sore had walked away with her lying in some dank dark alleyway and robbed of her money. The part about the loss of that money she brought her out of it. Those damned losers, she though with her utmost of distaste towards them. Their money was still in her jacket pocket.

She would never admit those losers caused the spotting on her, Velvet Bigouletti, sofa.

CHAPTER FOUR

The ten days and passed rapidly. A phone call every day from nurse Roberta kept the tediousness of dullness to just under overwhelming. He did the television which incorporated FM radio. He listened to the war of the worlds show done by W.K.B.W. Buffalo, New York station crew more than forty times and that closed his mind off from the dangerous situation he had landed into.

His short time taken in the first two days was totally unthought-of. He was always careful to handle such problems. The last time just before being diagnosed with the COVID-nineteen virus was no different. He handled it with precision. No witnesses. The only evidence was what he meant to leave. It would not lead to him, so he no longered himself with the aggravation that the police might easily arrest him here.

Do you have a place to go when you leave here? That question had been asked of him on three different occasions since he had checked into the hotel quarantine area. It was the sole thing that did depress him. Being asked that once was once too much. His reply to it the second time he kept to himself. I ought break your face. He forgot his reply easily enough. Shit, came from his voice box the third time. When questioned on his reply, he thought it better say nothing. He also thought it best to with the swiftness place his foot up her ass. Since it was all done by phone as not to spread virus that was not going to happen. He did not know who the people were who interviewed on his health every day.

No symptoms chose to attack him, so on the tenth day security were told that he could go home, so they escorted him on different path then the one he was escorted to his room on. Finally some real food.

It took exactly one day before he got to the understanding. Real food at this stage of COVID pandemic meant free sustenance from shelters and whatever other homeless resources there were. The riots had the grocery stores shut down. The laws closed the restaurants. If her had had family or friends he still would not have in pinged on them. They were in the same dirty as was he.

Nothing was open. He had slept in his apartment. Little food had been stored there as he had made up his mind months ago before the pandemic to forego cooking so he needed not to wash dishes. Now the restaurants that were his staple had been ordered and put out of serving by the Governor, Lousey freaking Democrat.

The last thing she wanted in her life was to go against today's societal norm, the news on the television changed her mind. The broadcasted program changing was one week earlier.

The girl been a student, at Simon Gratz, a ghetto neighborhood elementary school. The child was not in any of the classes she taught but she had seen her, noticed the child must be having home problems over those four years. She had kept her own council. Kept her mouth shut. Now the little red head was dead. Beaten to death.

The report stated the home was broken into. Invaded, robbed and the girl was the only one indoors at the time.

She had remembered her girlfriend and associate deaconess at: holy Blow founder, church telling her a guy who handled such things when the mother of an abused little one had not sufficient c__ hairs to have the authorities address the problems. Though the police were paid to handle such insufficiencies as child abuse, both physical and mental.

She sought him out. Save the child.

No answer at his door. There was a park nearby. Only three streets away. Remembering an insignificant piece of information, she pulled it together. His things he's a good father with those birds. Maybe she fed them as did most old guy gangsters in books and movies. None of the gangster molls even sat in a park distributing break crumbs and pieces of pretzels. She tried there a couple of days. No contact. On an occasion or two when there was no answer at his door, she sat in the park and by ordinance watched the people looking as bunch of bank bandits go by with their mouths and noses covered. There were some with the Seattle Supersonics logos on their face pieces. What are the words for them? Oh, yes. Masks. Masks wearing was legally mandated countrywide law. How the ones were found to fit the little children she noted none of us are truly safe. The girls wearing pink ones or lavender colored one. The boys with cowboy and super hero ones. Where are our female super hero masks she had a negative muse. Not happy in the least bit. Only enlightened. Blue on one side. White on the other side again she consorted that the little people seemed undiscomforted by those elastic bands behind the cars holding the protection stable. Unlike that of her own which pressed into the back of her ears without and appeasement to her own comfort.

Blliitt, Blliittt, Blliiitt. Hello. May I help you. He answered his cellphone. Hey guy. You alright man? Your mail is piling and some babe has been leaving you notes on your room door. Says she needs you to call her. Jethro? Yeah. Good to hear from you. I took a little when I came out of quarantine. I am in Philadelphia, Mississippi. You coming back anytime soon. I am not sure yet. Are you okay? Yeah I'm good. How's my girlfriend. Mitni is fine. She was worried a little about you. She's a great kid Jethro. Tell her I give her a shout. She'll appreciate that. What do I do about your mail and

The babes notes? Hold my mail for me, will you? You have the woman's phone number with you now? In my hand man here it is. Well wishes were given.

The two hung up their cell phones.

He kicked the unconscious villain smartly in his shattered teethed mouth with the suede steel toed, toe of his boots again that was the tenth time. Most of the teeth were now shattered his lips were the consistency of a much breakfast cereal. The four parts of his jaw bones had been shattered too. The boots had splinters of teeth and pieces of skin and flesh. They were also ruined with splotches of the victims sanguine fluid.

That job done, so before he departed two more vicious velocitied kicks with into the unconscious one's left eye. They were meant to blind that eye.

As he made his departure, the two hidden on lookers, one a six year old Asian girl, the other the child's mother. The mother is pleased. Her daughter's rapist has been the cost. The two went home from their incognito post, but first the parent stopped off at Ling's sweet Bakery and treated the little likeness and herself. Herself for getting the right man for the job. She really felt pleased with his work. The child had only talked to their hero for a couple of minutes two days ago.

Morality in this part of the world had fallen so deeply he was shocked by the reasoning he had been called in Mostly mothers of young children had no care to the rape of one or more of the offspring. They had begun to not only except the rapes but in a manner encourage them as long as an escape from their own responsibility to call the law on their child's antagonist did not land upon themselves. He looked up to that young Asian parent as his hero.

Four city blocks later in the middle of the one hundred forty block south Mitzorango way he enter the rental van.

Twenty miles away and two hours later a little boy Samuel Adams stood beside a small breasted, medium waistline super wide hipped Caucasian middle aged large rocked four carat diamond and thick wide platinum wedding ring. He gave the two a nod and two entered the econline.

Two days later the evening news reports a minor story on the break-in of the Blue county Zoo. The main gate door lock was broken and their liquor storage area was pilfered for eleven cases of alcohol.

What was never found was the extra meat the lions, tigers and leopards were fed. What was never found was the smile on his face at his musing the animals in captivity were again eating human flesh as their ancestors had done in the jungle while in the wild.

Both jobs he had been called in for were done. He was headed to the train station on his way back home to Seattle Washington.

CHAPTER FIVE

In Constitution county a suburd of Allerton Texas, Lorenzo "Lil L" Halftown almost exhausted returns to his minihacienda. Blood and both of his hands, trousers and eight thousand dollar stetso cowboy boots.

His normal routine through his adult years when returning home from a call was a sixteen ounce long neck bottle of Alabama full bodied black beer inundated will with crystals of ice. Frost on the exterior.

He would have had a couple double straight bourbons with his father a former US Marshall who died of lung cancer five years back. He was remembering those days and lied down. He fell to sleep straight away with the thought of tipping up a cold one unfulfilled.

Falling. Falling. Falling towards rapid eye movement his vision showed him a future.

She was barely moving. Had she been on her feet her knees both would be bent into angles. Her eyes both would be closed. Her arms stiff but angled as were knees. Her senses dulled to a near nilness. She was in a full heroin nod. One could place one's full flat hand on her posterior. Perhaps a minute or so later her mind may or her mind may not recognized and make a small body gesture of disobedience. She was in a full heroin nod. Her skirt loosely fitting and half, the top half of butt was fully uncovered. That she was either unaware of or could not cipher enough to rectify it, her heroine nod was in full form,

As he was beginning to comprehend what the vision was allowing his mind to see R. E. M. opened a window for the door to his vision had slammed tightly shut.

Eight hundred miles east a startled Milonya Trump held her arms riggedly outstretched. He bent legs muscles stealed and tight really little buttocks crammed closed and its usual soft spongy self hardened like rock.

Her head almost always as clear as a bell in the last two years went blank. She froze in a seventy eight degree room. Her swimming caught it. Years of practice with this woman since she a bit older than a toddler had not let miss any bodily action by her star aquatic student and hi board aerobatic diver. The two together had made Milonya a world class champion.

Everything went smoothly with the team except for that one hellish, horrific year when her champion-to-be lost her ever-loving-mind and fell for Herriberto, Herriberto Sanabria, that Puerto Rican, lousey fuk who somehow got her to put that damned spike in her arm.

General knowledge tells us a split second in the measurement of time only is fast. But like a limit in time there is no limit of what can and does happen in a split second.

A small child, a girl, fearless yet unknowing climbs an eight foot ladder about to attempt her first high dive. She has been well trained and well coached. That in her bikini swimwear is a vigilant guard in attendance at the pools edge where the diver still above is to make her submergence.

On the scene of the divers practice session is her publicity agent, M Rodney Paul Banks. Banks is a successful publish author. He has had fifteen of his books published.

In that same split second the diver froze he has had an enlightening joyous epiphany. That ought to get her he decided.

He was thinking of Morrell McCarrells, his second divorced wife.

I can let her catch me watching my three-d television shows while lying on the floor right under the screen. She's smart and will tell me stop trying to look under the dresses of females in the movie. She is that way. She could never keep that to herself. Away from me it has to hit her that I cannot see what's under the dresses of the televised females anyway, Idiot!!

But I'll keep letting her catch me doing it. I'll get her attention over and over. She probably will even throw her hands up in surrender. Still I'll keep her catch me at it.

Once I have her total attention, she'll start to peep around the corner before she passes by the projection room. That is when I'll be sure I have her. Banks count not help but smile. No facial expression though. None other than that one looking like the kitty that ate the aviary pet.

Then I'll abandon those actions and get my video recorder. Soon enough I will, said with conviction, catch her trying to lie on the floor to see if she could possibly have been wrong about what I may have seen lying there.

I can see her now taking out the three-d television three-d glasses. Checking-up on me.

That's where the cam-recorder comes in.

All that is necessary for this deviousness to be accomplished is I have to invent a pair of three-d television glasses.

Bank also was a successful inventor. The books made him a multiple deca millionaire. His three inventions made him a billionaire.

His hobby was arranging for his daughters futures they had chosen for they are reachable.

His oldest daughter's split-second of hesitation had ended and she began to spring the diving board.

He did again suppress that old feeling of fear. The one he had gotten that day. The day he had attended her practice. She was ten years and neither his daughter nor her diving trainer had thought to apprise him, to warn him of her next step in training that had been taught to her two months before that fateful day.

Two months earlier to that practice.

Now Liebshen for your next lesson. One that will serve you well. First. As all ways I would progress to this step should you not be ready to except. Normally when you dive you as I have taught you reach the depth of the pool to where the force of your dive expires and you arch your frame and approach the surface, and when your surface you take on air. It is the humane and the correct procedure. No?

Now that you are ready I will introduce to you a friend.

Once your body reaches the point to where your submergence no longer is forced into the pool you're the weight and your, dive, do not arch upward. Do not arch upward to reach the surface; rather kick your two legs. Go deeper into the water. Touch the bottom and push off the floor of the pool to gain momentum. Come to the surface and do not forget whom you had just such a short couple seconds ago shook hands with. My friend is the bottom of the pool? Replied her student. Ja, liebshen.

He had almost dived into the pool that day.

He had taken only two steps towards his daughter when he saw her surfacing. He was angry until she emerged and in a triumphant cry with both fist raised and total glee in her face. We did it!!, did he began to calm and see her training had progressed. His heart would still beat. Her mother would allow him entry again tonight he mused-somewhat. He had been the chooser of her coach and teacher.

Forward back to the present.

When practice was done he kissed her his usual I love you infinity on her forehead.

Before he left she went to the shower.

She and the coach left the gym and there the two of them were. Big as day. The billboard across the street from the gym's front door on three large poles it showed the phot of a man's back. He was well dressed. The backs of his celebrity boots polished to a patent leather gleam. His right forefinger cupped by a little hand. That hand attach to two and a half foot beauteous smile on her face turned to look behind her. She in patent leather flat footwear, ankle socks with lace, a flowered dress knee high and two pigtails with a negro league baseball cap turned around backwards. The billboard phot-shops a trip to the Bentley. Bentley is still an auto of prestige. The little girl is Menmeth, her little sister and the man had only a short period of time left her with in the gym's pool area with a I love you infinity smooch.

Only three hours past he had passed out from near exhaustion. He had three unrelated dreams in that time, neither had any things to do with the other two. He remembered none of them as soon as they ended. Fate on occasion is not fickle. He was soon to be awakened. He would soon see the face of one of the dreams main characters. The doorbell rang.

CHAPTER SIX

L ockdown, a phrase used by the occupants and authority figured from the top position, warden to the secretary who answered her phone calls.

Dallas Federal Penitentiary, a mid-level security penal institution had been locked down for seventy two hours.

In a prison lockdown no inmate or prisoner as some would is then was allowed to leave the cell. The shower and medical calls were the only exceptions.

There was one other exception. Lockdowns were supposed to prevent this one but on this day lockdown purpose was ineffectual.

Count was being made. There were two hundred six inmates in this block. Three guards made the count of the prisoners. Should there have been no lockdown only two guards were used.

As soon as count started in the very first cell where two inmates were incarcerated there was to be only one, as Brook Adams, in for a three to five bit on petty theft charges was the reason for the lock down. Adams along with three others doing time but from a different block on the prisons opposite side had been murdered while in the yard.

The count stopped at very first cell. Lying on the floor was Pervial Ambergarten Jones. Three puddles of blood lye under his body. Blood had gushed from the back of his head. His body flat and faced down had a larger puddle under his abdomen to his left side. The last and most prevalent of the pools of blood was settled from the soaked area of his crotch.

Connectional office Leonara Bentley went back to the hood were the on duty CO's office is. She sounded the alert for the Gorilla Squad.

And then she hit the medical alert. No physician in a case as this were allowed to enter an inmates sleeping area without the seven C.O. Gorilla Squad.

These are ones no one inmate wanted to fend off. They all were over six feet six inches tall. They all were over three hundred eighty five pounds. They all came with steel batons and steel toes boots. They all were merciless. As a group Warden Charlene Shirley gave them all the "go" signal. She stood behind them figuratively one hundred percent. She alone had handpicked them. Of course had she stood behind physically, then all of her four foot ten and one half inches in height and he one hundred one pound frame would be totally invisible. Also she was never without her American Eagle, fifteen shot hand gun nine millimeter.

One could easily but should never misjudge that soft skinned, soft smile, soft narrow lips cherub like angelic face. She would put a group of holes in one's head if she had even the slightest provocation. The biggest rumor on her was she had another nine in an ankle holster.

Follow procedure. I will be in forty five minutes. Charlene told her guests with apologies the night would have to end early, right this minute even

Her six guests reclothed themselves. Two females pursed their assorted apparatus's. Gave their regretful sorrows. Said they were having a swell time and the fun loving socialite disappeared, in her place was a four star uniformed prison warden.

The last three things she did before approaching her Hummer in the garage was to holster her waist nine millimeter put on her left ankle desert eagle and lastly put on her right ankle desert eagle nine millimeter.

The garage door went up and humming H2 well out the electronic eye opened gate. She was gone.

On her way a curiosity struck her. The in Ukraine. Ukrainian Americans are sending Ukraine aide in supplies, money and have gone to Ukraine to fight against Russia. They are than in fact fighting to kill Russians, so what are the Russian Americans doing for their heritage country?

What will the American President do should Russian Americans fight against the ethnical war the American president has approved? Russians are Americans. Will he arrest them as the Japanese were during World War Two? And if he does, then how will that play.

Her Russian prisoners bleeped into her real of awareness.

Things were bad. They got even worse the next morning. She had showed in her office shower. The odor of the night before gave way to a hint at her personal. She needed to walk the prisons floor. Get a feel of what. All she knew was four murders had happened. One while in lockdown where no one could get a prisoner without the prisoner's cell door being unlocked. The prisoner also was in the cell alone. The next part she hated, it was a question. Two words only. The guards? Body smelling fresh and of lavender perfume she was about to press the intercom and order Zythe Mendell her secretary for this week to call up her body guards to escort. She was tough as pig-iron, but being smart as the process that turned coal to diamond she would not go alone. Plus it was prison procedure.

Her buzzer rang her first.

Deputy Warden Wallace on the line warden

Yes Wallace? Bad news! We have an escape.

CHAPTER SEVEN

Three days ago.

So the next few hours are going to bring one heck of an ice storm. This storm was totally unexpected. It should start in the next fifteen minutes to half an hour.

One hour later.

The news band glides across the television screen. The surprise ice storm that was supposed to happen did not form.

The next news band read, the body that was found in abandoned warehouse that was being rigged with explosives for implosion has been determined to be Frederick Glasni. His identity was found through dental exams and fingerprints.

The television program continued without further interruption.

A tear rolled out of an eye. Then another and another. By the time the fourth tear came both eyes began to run as two dripping faucets.

Three days later.

Whose missing asked the warden? The answer ran a chill through her. That same type of chill still clung to the deputy warden. Evan Glasni.

CHAPTER EIGHT

From the news of the dead body in the abandoned warehouse he made a phone call, that was yesterday.

The seven forty seven landed in Maple view. He had taken no luggage, only stuff his pockets with Franklin's and Grant's, a total of two hundred six thousand dollars.

The twenty BMW picked him up. Your weapons and ammo are in the truck when you are done dump this car. He knew that meant clean of any evidence that any one who had been in it would be identified.

He dropped the deliverer off and slowly rode out.

CHAPTER NINE

The police came late. There were broken table, pieces of wooden bar chairs, a hinge was buster it's top screws bent yet holding a hanging door. He had gone leaving those he asked of information who had denied him alive but sorry he took them on. He arrived in Maple view only an hour ago.

The restaurant owner gave the word to the two district officers a neighbor had called. This was a family squabble. Two brothers over one of their wives. The officers removed themselves reporting the 911 call unfounded and a couple hundred dollars a piece richer. The truth was he had gone to work seeking information on who it was that took the life away from the son of a friend. He was one of the boy's two godfather's.

The place looked organized. There were two sitting in chairs at outside tables there was food in front of each. It sat there for never an hour. The second floor window blinds moved occasionally but only a slit at each movement and always the same venetian rib. He decided to ask only one of them. One on the inside. He went through the front door grabbed a bottle of way, paid for it and began an exit. At the front door pff, pfft. No more outside guards. Turning nine more pfft's then he quietly strode up the stairs.

The hallway on the second story had one door. It was open and he shot her right in her back into the spine just above her crack of her buttocks. "she went rigid. Her entire body locked and then hit the carpeted throw roglimply.

She answered the only question he had to ask. He chose to accept it pfft pfft, into her head and he split.

On the way from the front door he shot a glance at who looked to be inappropriately dressed for the style in that area, as was he, not a clue to his partner. The second godfather.

That very night their paths crossed one another again. Gunfire raged inside auto manufacturing plant. The plant was closed due to presidential order in the effort to contain the spread of the pandemic.

The meeting was called by the three major business organizations in the state. All were suspicious of the others doings in the murders that had happened in the last twenty four hours.

The meeting just started when numerous explosions were heard. The business startled guns appeared and roaring automatics begin riddling the plush office and some had time to seek cover from injury a couple took hits.

More explosions were heard. Again the booms heard were outside the manufacture plant. Their outside security was being blow apart. They thought treachery among themselves. This meeting had been immediately called profit was at stake.

Something had happen. The heads of the organizations sought ways to retreat to escape the flying cop killers. They had been hoping for their guards outside to enter and assist in their cowardly retreats. None of outside lookout, body guard henchmen were able to.

The ammunition inside was depleted.

Fear of death forced the sides to flee seven men of the twelve were alive and retreated. All three sides found their guards dead and every automobile decimated. Burning. They had to retreat on foot. The seven who ran in all directions were found dead. Gunned down. They were scattered. Investigation told they died in numerous spots. None closed the a football field's distance to one another.

The godfather found dead bodied that he had not finished off.

I have help. Each came to that conclusion.

In the message parlor and two thousand dollars out of his pocket and into the pardons cash register he had been lying still on his back half of his on the bed. His legs hanging over feet flat on the floor. He had fallen asleep almost as soon as he lied down.

The deal he had made with Mommasan was still being kept.

Her knees were on the folded comforter. She was totally nude. Totally engrossed in carmine her way. Her hair held back by the scrunchie. As she began to tire, so went deeper on him. Opening up wider because the deal was for her to not release him, so before going to sleep herself she also with her mouth engulfed his testicals along with his meat-rod. Secure should she sleep as she had the feeling she would the package would not escape her oral chamber. She shortly slumbered.

Going along Ben Gazzra Way, his attention was taken away from his present duty. There stood a little boy about nine perhaps ten years old. What caused him to stop and pull over to the curb was that look on her face. He had seen hundreds even thousands of times before.

As he got out of the rented roadster, he gave her the old ahem. No notice of it from her, so he gave her an even louder harrumph. That gave way to her and she turned he head towards his approach.

She once the three of them spoke to one another informed her that he was not a policeman, but rather a citizen who handle the child's plight.

She took him home and called up to an upstairs window. Bellamy opened it, she become and Bellamy came to the front door. He was standing in the shadows.

I'm going to the police. By the time I get back I want you gone or what you've been doing hero is gonna put your ass right in jail. What I been doing to Leeroy. He took step towards. She stepped back pulling the child along with her by the shoulder of his polo shirt. I ain't done shit to Leeroy he gritted. You have too, said the boy. Boy I ought tuh. She pulled her child a further away. Past the alleyway. Get out of my apartment she threaten said to him. Again she stepped back pulling little Leroy with then she feigned a turn suggesting the two would be on their.

Threatened he launched a himself towards their pretended retreat. Both she and the oy ridgedly flintched and she grabbed son and put up an arm to protect them from outstretched arm. He did reach them.

Instead a surprised child rapist and would be assaulted was forcefully yanked from behind off his feet into a dark alleyway between the two houses.

The noise of the attack did not last long, maybe fifteen seconds, then came pfft. Pfft. Pfft. The black small figured mother made a correct assumption a silencer from a pistol had just gone off.

The stranger emerged from his dark hideout. Your problems are over. He kneeled in front of the boy. Never allow that to happen to you without telling your mother to call the police and report it. We have men doing jail time and some of the prison police who will handle such types of people. He looked in the mother's eyes. She looked into his, as he said to the boy. Promise me. Leroy gave his promise.

The no longer a complete stranger to them began to stand straight but in a crouch he remembered the fullness of the routine, and Leroy, he said softly yet solemnly you are never to do that to a child, boy or girl. Become a MGA, a good and get you a woman. An adult for your exploits. Promise me. I promise.

Then he became erect. The woman held onto the forearm she had latched herself to and guided him upstairs. He, the man had taken awareness that she had peered into the alleyway while he took the oaths from her son and saw the offensive boy could not be seen.

To the woman and her child the world just got a retrieval.

CHAPTER TEN

The shuttle according to the National Aviation Space Administration reports the Air Force Quest launch last week while testing its new hyper speed coil performed to well. For greater than anticipated. When set in launch it was supposed to richocette around the planet Mars then be shut down and rendezvous with the Russian controlled International space station.

When launched it went into a speed not anticipated and in less then three minutes left our solar system and in a half hour has departed from out Milky Way Galaxy.

It is confirmed too that all of Earth's tracking satellites have lost communication and there has been no contact.

We switch now to Mac Humper is Spain where the communication was recorded.

The biggest news story in history and the couple never heard a word a word from the set. The child who had been rushed off to bed to give his mother and her newly found protector a bit of space for him to accept her appreciative... stood in his partially opened bedroom door and viewed the news broadcast.

Her bedroom door had closed for over an hour. He could not have heard even if the bedroom door had been left open. Her thighs covered and nullified all sound from both of his ears.

Both god fathers had been in the same condition until daybreak the next morning.

That day break brought on his departure the television still on had a commercial that gripped him into a momentary stillness.

The governor of the state stood there on the screen. Four uniformed police officers stood silently in still motion.

Thank you. Said the governor for allowing my bill to become law. Now no child or child's parent have any reason not to bring the molester and in some cases molesters of a child whether uncle, aunt, any other family member or a parents live-in mate to get away with breaking the law of child molestation. There is now no statute of limitations on the crime of child molestation. We take credit for this legal action. Yet we give credit to a governor in the state of Pennsylvania for the attempt, though it to date has been only an attempt to raise the age of the molested victim to be raised from their own age of thirty five too the age of fifty as an age was his proposed statue of limitations in that state.

That was a good thing the god father said to the woman he was about to leave. Yeah. That commercial has been ordered by our governor to come on at least once a day everyday and at various times. He said in his first one he wanted to get the message to all of us. That one was on three or four times a day for about three months until he got his bill made into a law.

Crazy thing those commercials were paid for by the top ten businesses in the country. She kissed his neck with her flicking tongue and both hands on his panted crotch.

Still he had work to do.

Just hours later a news update told of a center city business district's traffic being detoured. A well multimillionaire and owner of tallest building in the had been murdered. He was found on the entrance way to his buildings private parking lot. His head had been blown from his neck. Presumably the weapon was a shotgun. His chauffer been shot in his forehead through the limo's front windshield. There were no witnesses. More at ten.

The business just yesterday had been freed on bail of seven hundred fifty thousand dollar cash bail. He had been arrested on the charge of child sex trafficking.

When the on scene criminologist was allowed to view the crime scene he munerted a hint of soy sauce was in the air. None was discovered on any physical surface. The aroma would linger and present itself here and there at times to come.

His cell he had kept on. WKBW radio station out of Buffalo New York still broadcast in these days. As it should be.

It was the most talked radio show of all time back in the day. Back in the day he caught himself. That day my moms was only three years old. Her folks, probably had her hacker in that late at night. Smiling. At least she got to see the Jean Peters, Gene Barry movie war of the worlds based on that back in her day radio show. Hmph. Base or the HG Wells book. Those thoughts went so quickly he had more time less at the stop traffic light to tune in his download of the radio program remake on his phone. The only cause he ever kept his phone on when doing a job.

Ladies and gentlemen, this is Dan Neverette, the program began.

Again a smile. Though Dan Neverette had died years back his son carried on his memory of that self same radio broadcast remake.

She was going to make him breakfast before he pulled up. Instead he left twenty Grants on her kitchen table. The alnight pharmacy. He pulled over. Toothpaste, toothbrush, dental floss, mouth wash and a bottle of water.

Behting wat, is my choice. Belting War it is. Now for the last detail but a poignant one. Should you care for floral arrangements we will need your specification. Type, color and quantity. The customer held her words. She did however take note of the funeral parlor's director's use of arrangements rather than arrangement, her use of the word quantity being suggestive of more than what could be used and or should be used. She kept to being calm though her seething rage mounted. She had to hold the woman only doing he job. She was doing what she is paid to do. She was only working on providing for her family as she herself has, had always done. Not anymore, her son's dead. She had no more family. Her line was ending with her. The funeral directory had not done this this thing to her. If only his father were here in stead of. If his were not in prison. If only you were here.

At the funeral arrangement meetings end the cost was paid in cash. Forty six thousand nine dollars eight cents.

She a thirty female counted the eight cents out first. True this is payment for her only child's funeral. Still may as well hold onto as much money as long as she could.

Mackenna Johnsen walked her to her car. He kissed her and hugged her. You going to be alright getting home hon? Sure I just want to sit here for a minute. Johnsen waited until she felt able to drive safely then he got on his Harley and went back to his office.

Benjamin Franklin middle school has a young slender Asian science labs teacher. He has died his hair a different color each in the reasoning students would physical and chemical change with the coloring of is defiantly. A visual teaching aid.

Twenty six students around bunson burners acids and other materials forces his attentions to be its highest at all times in the laboratory.

He pays very close attention to all of his students in all of his classes. Today he had taken note that Bobby, his given name, Robert Guess, is not only paying acute attention in class but for the only time to date four months plus into the school years is without prod participating in class.

He has summised but holds it no steady solution that his home abusal must have ended. He is right in his summization. The abuse has stopped. Tonight in the teachers home while lounging he will find the child's antagonist has been murdered. However he will not know if for sure and he will not associate the two.

CHAPTER ELEVEN

Even Glasni held court hundred times in his earlier years. Only once had he found his prey he was paid to assign a penalty of death did he not allow execute the sentence. He was well know by his fifth year in business. That one time he hid his face from his prey he found no fault in the boy and executed the payee of the hit.

Some only a sparsity tried to call him fair. Truth was fair had nothing to due with him changing the sentence. The boys father paid Glasni ten times the amount Glasni had been paid to cancel the young sprites life.

Even Glasni twenty years to arrest on any charge. Problem was his only arrest resulted in a ten years sentence. In his year he walked out. He could have within his first six months. He had figured out how.

The news broadcasted the finding of a dead body in abandoned warehouse. He paid little attention, hardly enough to give it a thought later that same day.

Hey Glasni, Pondurance a, lifer times three called to him as Glasni's cell was being passed. Pondurance had faked an illness. He was hoping to leave with Glasni.

Yeah Glasni answered. I know you get a plan on how to get outta here. I'll pay you my debt you take me with you.

I am not leaving for another two if I keep out of trouble Pondu, but yes you are right if I chose to leave out of here I do have a way. He was surprised. Pondurance would know that much about him. Even with his convictions Pondu as Glasni, called him, not many dared to, was a wise guy. Crooked Nosed, you understand.

Even though some scum sucker killed yo kid?

What are talking of Pondurance? Your kid they found him dead in an empty warehouse. Been on the TV all day.

CHAPTER TWELVE

The escape of Glasni hit the aire. There was evidence on how he had gotten out of the medium secure prison. His escape took a backseat to report that he had escaped at the same time as the life times sentence Elipse Pondurance a well known organized crime hitman.

The search was on for Pondurance and Glasni.

It was reported that Glasni's son had recently been found dead and televised and that that broadcast is more than likely to have made Glasni and model prisoner until the newscast assist Pondurance in his escape.

Mrs. Hennie Yun was the wife of Ji Li Yuan, a purveyor of automatic, semi-automatic hand guns and shot guns. He was the owner of his shop Yun Weapons. Yun arrived at shop, it was already open as usual. Yun employed two people at each of his two hundred Yun Weapons worldwide dealerships.

Meazzy Smythe an Eglishter as Cole Partar called his origin was the senior of the two employees.

Good morning sir said Smythe. Good morning boss said Partar. Good morning guys Yun returned. Everything okay here? Asked you. The usual Smythe came back with.

Yun's office phone rang. It Jeet Kun Yun, the oldest son named after the art of self defense developed by a legendary Chinese Kung fu master.

The conversation went on casually but before it ended Jeet said to his dad I talked to you for a while very casually because I was ordered to do so. I am on speaker. We are being held as hostages. This is want our captors want from you.

Then a strange voice came over his houses land line. That's all I require. As soon as you bring them to me your family and you are free from this.

Mezzy you guys can leave an hour so early today. Cole I need you to secure a couple of items.

Yun and Cole went into the store room. Yun gave Cole a short list. I'll need these at eleven fifteen. Cole surveyed the list. You got boss. It was ten thirty, close to anyway.

Three thirty PM the gun shop closed.

Two hours earlier the police sent a detective and three uniformed officers, one of them the field supervisor were in the Yun household.

The supervisor held the rank of corporal. He in ranking outranked the detective and had charge of this ongoing case if he chose to.

He had my family as hostages. You better believe I gave him what he wanted. If you love your family, you do the same.

I am not arguing with you Mr. Yun. Nor am I saying you did anything wrong. Just putting down what you and your family tell me.

All you gave to him was three sets of guns. All three fifty seven magnum with interchangeable barrels. Those barrels were twelve, ten, eight, six and four inch barrels. Also each of the three sets had all those interchangeable barrels in each set. You also gave him the tool kits to change the barrels, each changing kit came with each magnum set. Lastly the ammunition was ten cases, forty shots per case, all the ammunition was Teflon coated. Have I got the list correct? Yes. But he also had me give him two dragon scale vest. Bullet proof. I'll make sure I put that down.

The detective asked the supervisor, you got anything to ask that may help us here? You're on point.

Glasni was gone. He had kept to the script that kept him from prison for so many years. Three pair of surgical gloves. Face mask. Athletic mouth protector. No finger prints. No facial recognition. Verbal disguise. The other measure(s) are top secret. He was gone clean.

The kidnapping did not remove the two escaped prisoners from the news TV screen completely but it did cut down their usual two or three minutes a day down to thirty seconds two or three times a day.

Glasni slept on the pavement outside of an all filled shelter for the homeless. He kept to himself. But the billboard directly across the street held off his sleep for hours. He did not know why the ad disturbed him so much. Could his son have been raped too along with being murder and discarded in such a manner?

Has your child been raped? In big red letters on a white billboard. At the middle of the ad. Turn in the rapist even if it is a family member or your, sex, partner, was put in the ad under, loved one, that a line was drawn threw.

At the bottom was inked, either you or the rapist is going to get busted. Save the babies!!

He must have been only half unconscious in his sleep because not wanting to be identified he covered his face each turn.

CHAPTER THIRTEEN

The godfather were equally like minded. Though one got the news of Glasni's freedom hours before the other. Each in turn within seconds of the news knew. Both thought the exact same two word phrase. He's here.

They knew of Glasni. Glasni did not know they were in town.

Glasni was pretty sure no one other than he knew the two of them knew him. No one alive knew the two were his son's grandfather's, so once there since he could not contact the young man's mother for information. The feds were sure to on the look out for him here. He called Jason Jatum. No answer. Then he called thee Bundy. No answer. A second of concern. The television news report hit him. I saw it. They are here. Three bulbs now burned bright. Like there tempers they all burned hot with hatred. If the s-o-b's weren't dead already than they soon would be.

Hello Miss. May I ask you one question. My son was just buried. I know. That is why I flew twenty five hundred miles. Slightly confused and suspicious but no questions. I am here because his father would want me to be here. I don't know you and his father's in prison, so do not lie to me. Ma'am. I am you son's godfather. His father is no longer in prison. G, broke out last.

A few feet away a stranger stood still and quiet and thinking of clacking open a skull. The second godfather still held his stand. His mind heard. His mind went into attack mode. Then his mind thought, he's here.

I will get in touch with you soon. Even would want me to help out with you expenses. Please except this. The ten grand was in a yellow business envelope. He decided then and there. See if I can trust her. When you even, say I said hello. Say I stopped in and gave my respect. He walked away. The Corvette door had closed. He would not have heard her call out and ask what his name was except the Vet's drop-top was folded away. He pointed the envelope and left.

Repat Roera, is the greatest written of short storied in this century. His books have sold over three quarter billion copies in the past eleven years. The have yielded nine big screen motion pictures grossing six billion dollars over all. Some of his characters have been made into action figures with accessories and again yielding in the deca-billion dollar range.

Today his release from state prison is being televised. All of his novels were written while he was the guest of the prison system in the Republic of Brazil.

He owes no time to the government as far as parole. He did do all of his time he was sentenced to. He in convict terms, maxed out.

Mevat Lashist is there to greet him at his arrangement. Lashist is the highest charging and most successful prostitute in South America.

They immediately process by chauffer driven Bentley limo to the airport and the private he has arranged to take them to North America.

His youngest nephew of seven years of age had been getting sexually molested. He has a need to comfort his sister, talk to his nephew and appease North America of the breathing of air of childhood rapists, since the laws in America do not cover the spectrum of his sister's complaints.

One the jet. Ahhh. Regular eats.

Fresh clothing. Citilian gators. Electric razor. Platinum, white jade and rhinestone, rings watch, bracelet and neck chain, all he adorned after he and Mevat took care of the natural calls of one released from an all male prison over a long period. This was mainly to allow Mevat to believe she was doing an astronomical deed. Reality had shown since his writings in his second year of incarceration had made him not only a star but a rich star the female guards had been earning a thousand dollars two or three times every week.

Through those satiated years he held to one desire. He added it to his to do list. Once this trips business is concluded he will return to Brazil to seek an affair with both the wardens and assistant warden's wives.

His mind was a bit perturbed. His release a couple minutes ago could Mevat have caused that one?

The thought he held in his mind. What do those wives look like? That inquiry stabbed at his brain over and over. Perhaps to get ease of mind is why he chose to have the auto's chauffer pull over in order that might find the reason for the gathering of people listening to the high yellow complexioned speaker on the podium. He had no reason to do so. His sister and nephew were the direction he was traveling, yet he stopped. He listened. He heard.

The speaker barely took notice of the two seeking his message that had just exited the Bugati.

Speech continued and the only in the car with J.F.K. in the back seat was his at that time wife Jackie B. Kennedy. On the thirty foot high projection screen used for showing movies outdoors showed the reason for his opinion.

As the former president's head rest on his chest from being shot in the back of his head, his at that time wife Jackie turns sideways towards him places her left hand under his chin resting on his chest and pieces of flesh, brain and the top of his skull bone burst upward into the air. Quickly as though from force his head is flung upward and backward.

The only way this could have happened by gunshot wound as reported the second shot did to him is if Jackie Kennedy had the apparatus that tired that second shot. The video of the assassination shows it plainly. Why then if I realized it, and you can see did the Central Intelligence Agency not pick it up. Its right there in front of our eyes. That is why I had the movie stopped where our former president was shot both times?

I will not pause here because there is more to see. As the video progressed with a later pointer he showed the assassinated president's wife crawing out of the back of the car where the president was assa- no I am going to interject murdered here where she comes in contact with what was supposed to be secret service agent who was at that point on top of the trunk of the president's transport.

Here again the video stops showing Jackie and a reported SS agent both on the car's trunk. Then it is played on to see the agent get off the car and leaves. The wife of the president calmly gets back into the back seat of the car. Where by the way the president has just been murdered. Why?

Why did the SS agent not take her away from area being shot into as if he knew she would be safe?

Ladies, gentlemen, citizens I leave you with this. That assassination, murdering a president of the United States of America was over fifty years ago. To this date no one who saw what you just saw and being in position to right our children wrongly taught nor even attempt to bring the governmental guilty to trial. Why?

You saw it. I saw it. This is our country. Why are we powerless to do so?

The couple took glances around. Then with urging, a slight urge from Roera, Mevat leaves with him to re-enters the Bentley.

CHAPTER FOURTEEN

Are you one of superstitious values? I myself am not. Still for this book I will not put to paper the reputational unlucky number thirteen. To be blunt, no chapter thirteen will ever by my own hand be in this publication.

The Friar was a new man to him. One he had not been in the past acquainted with. His former life is why he approach the Franciscan. Mass had ended and as Friar Joseph Mole, was leaving the room above the food distribution located over the offices on the floor below in order to head to his living quarters across the street on the even ending number of the block where he would come out of his duty robe a man he had never met, yet- he seemed so similar.

Friar, he spoke to the priest, may I have a solemn few words with you?

I see no reason not to. Is it immediately important? Or, can you wait about ten minutes while I go home and change? Realizing the stranger and her had never met, I live right across the street. Faher it is important. I hope it may take only a few minutes. Please? Shoot your breeze says friar mole.

This will have to be in the order of a confession. Okay? The priest says his few words of assurance.

Before you tell me, I do recognize you. I saw your phot on the free neighborhood paper.

Good. My confession will not take so long. I have escaped prison for a reason. I am here to find out who murdered my boy. Don't know if he made that paper but a couple days ago he was found dead in the old abandoned candy warehouse. I saw it on the news after an inmate told me. I am going to kill who did it. That is my confession. Please say a prayer for my son and is mother and for me.

I was going to do my time and come home father but now...

Blessing are given except for the part of the intentional murder. That was explained. The two parted ways.

CHAPTER FIFTEEN

We look like this. Thanks for registering in your own name. It made it easy to find you. You come across any news for me? You find out yet who took my kid out?

You know I got busy soon as I heard. Munch, the boy's nickname, got real lucky having two godfathers. Yeah. I figured if either of you got his, he would someone to look out after him. Figured I would need the – hey both of you here? Seen him taking to Munch's mom. Introduced himself to her. Trying to get info I guess. Don't think he did.

Think we should go get him? No. That train wrecker is a stone cold loner. Dependable as day and night, twice as loyal and tour times deadlier than he is loyal. Just like you, if he finds out who did that he'll go home. He finds out I broke out he will stay away from my family.

I'm tired of talking lets move man. This may be your home town, but I say we paint its sky bloody til Munch's murderer is in the dirt. Good move. Let's go.

The two went in different directions.

Leaving the monk. Robert Orton. Killed your boy entered his mind. The message was received in his mind as a truth. He knew that such notations were sent out to a person. On most such occasions the person the cipher was sent to was also admitted to others brain receptors. One usually did not know who else was delivered.

He kept his reply of gratitude for after verification.

This being an escaped prisoner was awkward to him. None of his known contacts could be used.

The forty five godfather number one had given him accompanied only two full clips outside of the one loaded into the grip of the gun his shirt completely camouflaged. He had surprised his backup so no other arrangements were set to get more. Basically this city, his city was a nude baby he had just met.

Later that night while talking to God Friar Robert Orton says to God, in my own heart I must confess I wish to tell convicted criminal who has escaped from prison on the only purpose of the taking away the life of the man who murdered his son even though he unlike myself does not yet know who raped and murdered the boy. Both men told me of their lives. One past and one future. You will intercede and see to it that justice is done? That was the question of the night.

Your word demands the rapist death via man to boy. May lying man as he does with woman is an sin punishable by death. The father by your law has the right to put the sodoniser to death and I cannot tell the father because I learned of the abomination in the confession. Sanity must abide.

You put something in my way, so should I put to death the abominable sinner, will you still go up to the deed with me?

After that talk the monk desired some fresh air and Molly White pulled closer to the cemented walls surrounding the entrance to the house two doorways down the block. The man who had been walking the through the area looking for a quickly found her easily. He looked out while she stooping gave a half-ass performance. The friar was not new to this neighborhood. The two years since he had been transferred here from Philadelphia, Mississippi showed him that drug addled areas and hookers have mush in common.

The guy Molly was per scoping with has what the hung like a horse group would call a embryo sized dick. That aspect of his body was not an odd tiring with one exception. His biological father was one of those guys with a very big cock. You would say his father a hung like a horse group. His tiny four and a half inch stiffy was a trait of the males on his mother's side.

His father on the birth of his son was a ninety nine plus percent positive the two were father and son. Molly swallowed his member fully with a laughable ease.

Since he paid he a hundred dollars she did not come off of it until his ejaculation and both departed happily. He back home to regret Iris miserable living single existence bring alone again. She directly to her peoples crack house slash shooting gallery and called out to Brooklyn the neigh hood crack dealer on that four to midnight shift.

Ahh. The night air felt refreshing. On his way to the all night seven Twelve, a rip off of the major food chain store he saw Brooklyn handing out a couple of samples.

The monk had seen the scene in all of the Ghetto areas in all the major minority areas in all the cities he had been assigned and to date he could not fathom the truth why illegal drug sales exist. The police had in all those places bee aware of the illegality and the illegal law breakers on both sides pushers and buyers.

Some day he tried to think. The law will do its job fully. He prayed to God for forgiveness for thinking a false witness.

Lunch proved to be as unsucculent as a flat tire. Do not blame the service not blame the cook. The service usually good became excellent. The matribee recognized her. He told the waitress whose table the women would be seated. You see that woman in the pink tight slacks that was said. Not spoken as a question. She is the mother of the kid found dead in the candy plant. I saw her on the news. Be at your absolute best. A message went to the chef. Do this order especially right. Everything precisely as ordered. The know Clemonton. Clemonto Morgosi, the matridee got the okay from is staff. So the service was polite to the point of being curtious beyond expectations. The food was the best ever served.

The mood of a mother's grief not yet sedated was at it's fulfillment. The meals were barely touched. Perhaps if the four females had known what the restaurant's workers had done to please them and to ease a mother's torment, then maybe the meal could have the detecting taste buds.

Two went to the lavatory to remove the shine from their noses. Although I never did know a few snoots of cocaine dust was how a proboscis was rendered an outbreak to dullness.

The mother told a third to go back to the car. She had forgotten something and needed it. The third female tiny tittiel, scrawny legged, very thin arms, thick unattractive eye glasses had a posterior the size of which would fat, fat woman envious. It was so huge then when she had sat down half or more spilled of the dinner tables chair seat.

The mother alone with the last one gave her a few words not seeing anger nor gleam from either of the ladies. The group let a total of two hundred in gratuity.

CHAPTER SIXTEEN

The entire country got the news and were in shock. When he escaped from prison as a hit man for organized crime nine out of ten people interviewed swore their opinion was he would be in an a extradition treaty country. He would only return to the US if a hit was ordered.

He had committed suicide late at night when cornered by the FBI. That type of suicide had become common in the latter years. Mostly for cop killers. Mostly.

The other story was the law no one knew was being pushed through by the Federal Transportation Advisory Board. It passed with only descending vote.

This law will make air travel more difficult for drug users and safer for all airline passengers and employees.

Test would be given to all passengers before boarding. The test is for illegal drug use. It a passenger or employee's test came up positive the user would be arrested immediately when the plane lands. The charge would be a felony. Illegal possession of narcotics.

FBI local office. So it's decided we have put the team was on our dead fugitive in charge of your fugitive. They got their man first, so as agreed they are on the jet landing right about now. Co-operate when they get here.

Chief inspector no contact has been made with his family or people he knew. Its been two weeks since he broke out. I know his kid being murdered set him off. He did not make the funeral parlor before the funeral, nor the viewing, nor the burial. His most likely going to stay away from here and a year or so from now he will make a mistake.

Chief I got a feeling he's here now. All he wants is to get perp who got his boy. The boys friends are under surveillance.

Then we have nothing yet. I think I will bring the new officers into this and request we keep a closer watch on the schools they went to. What about the kids girl friend? He had two. They apparently do not know one another not even about each other being the other.

Chief do we have any more news on the pedifities registered in the area. Since the boy was raped, I still think that is the best group to follow-up on.

He hasn't been to the morgue either, I think Harry and Thomas are on their shift now. You think? You know Harry sir, if he came up with something. Check!

That is it gentlemen and ladies.

A knock on the conference room too. A well dressed female agent's head pokes through the door. She gets an okay from Chief Agent Bifrost.

He got him chief. Questioning look crosses Bifrosts brow. It is in his eyes also.

The case you're meeting on. The boy's rapist. A one hundred percent match from both the anal semen and his oral swabs. The perps name is, Molasses Arigon. Lives right here.

He is in custody. Precinct One. Alert them. Agent Rivers and Agent Mendletown will be there. Tell them do nor transport him until after we interrogate him. Yes sir.

The very serious men met unscheduled outside of a police district and left out of it before the arrival of the FBI agents sent to be sure the prisoner was exactly what he was arrested for being.

The Feds walked inside the entrance went to the bullet proof glass window to show their identification and got enlightened. The police behind the glass in the office were unconscious.

Agent Mendletown picked the door. Everyone in the precinct was unconscious. They found the prisoner they had arrived in interrogate gone.

Somewhere across the Big Pond in England a security leak flows like olive oil around the planet. Curiously the leak comes in the form of a voice not unlike that of the Queen Mother. Nick, the voice goes, make sure our veterans are never mistreated in any manner. Those American veterans have been so distastefully miscared for by their Philadelphia Pennsylvania Regional office having their livelihood stolen by that regional office and their Congress, Senate and house of representation have done nothing to rectify' the financial instability. Perhaps we should not directly say so to the world's public but I have made a decision to hit their government in the side of the face with a slush hall. Make sure the statement I prepared personally gets publicity. We of England are appalled at ourselves and heartfelt fully apologize for the act of slavery.

Make certain mv forces are never treated so woefully as those veterans m the states.

The apology for slavery was broadcast worldwide but only South America was mention in the apology. You go girl.

That is what was the RV as the three tortured their captive. Never finding any reason, only that a female prostrated herself to have him do so.

Just before the prisoner was given a penectomy he gave them her name and place of employment. Then he was castrated his eyes gouged from their homes and his tongue after being cut out was violently shoved into his anus pore to block the seepage of alcohol and lighter fluid. The RV was doused fully with ten gallons of jet fuel and they left with it and him inside. A full blaze.

It was all over now. He did visit his son's mother. He did not visit his son's grave. He chose two very important mauvevers. Do not out her in the spot where she had to turn him in or be arrested herself. The second was as the first do not get caught. There work here done and all three now familiar with each other never saw one another again.

The reason starts in the next chapter.

CHAPTER SEVENTEEN

Four months three weeks five days six hours seven minutes eight seconds and one zeposecond from the date and time a three fifty seven hollow point went into the left eye of, Bitty Parker Schram, Longbow Scalper Riversend stepped off the passenger ladder of the Red bird seven fifty seven.

His tour in the Bolivian jungle ended in near disaster yet successful by the slimmest of margin.

He was given the news, old as it was that his son was dead, mutilated and burned to the point that one charred barely recognizable bone shard and ash remained.

That self same instant in time the President of the United States of America being on a state wide capital tour had just seconds before bit into a Nathanial's Chili dog with raw onions and mustard on a pretzel dough hot dog roll keeled over dead.

Starting to hail the next taxi cab in line, he was halted by a small hand placed fat on his bottom.

He was warmly in comfort where before the touch his heart eyes demeanor were as cold as dry ice.

Little Pearl, he quietly spoke with a loving tone that can easily be described as awesome.

He turned and she would have been there standing but Little Pearl Thunder storm the Saint Joseph's School for Lakota Apache orphaned children's owner was totally in love with Longbow Riversend and as he turned to see her she was already in the you looked on me mode and had lepy into the air wrapping her short arms around his neck. Her legs wrapped around his massive body and her lips were immediately accepted by his. The two were in love with each other over twenty years. She had a bond psychicly with him like no others on this planet. Where ever he was, whatever he did she always knew, even before the two first laid eyes on one another. She laid him that same day.

Her light heartedness assured him things were good.

The two walked to the parking area where her brand new fully equipped totally tricked out pink and white Hummer awaited. He drove.

Your equipment is in the back seat. One peace pipe. One torch. One piece of pipe. Let's go to the hotel first? There was the chance that Little Pearl had been with some other while he was away but it was not with me as he thought. He waited until a signal light caught them. While awaiting the color change her medium sized left hill breast was in his palm was kissed through her blouse.

To the rental the went.

Baby that was good and I figured I better some fast. How soon you going to leave. Its just that you just got back. I sure would like more home time but for some reason I have been feeling you have a reason to not come home.

You here on the news about the boy that got found her in a candy company's closed building. No, I don't think so. I heard the news was on for days. Oh, yeah maybe this will ring a bell. The child's mother a week later was murdered. Shot in her eye outside of her job. She was a clerk in this city's capital building. She was the boys mother, yeah I remember that. There is no easy way to tell you. The woman was on assignment with me. The kid was my son. No way I could lie to.

He never got to finish that sentence. She grabbed her truck keys and left as she went out of the door she gathered her clothing. Her panties, bra and tennis shoes she put on in the hallway after she closed the suite's door.

CHAPTER EIGHTEEN

Call off the troops. We found the killer. He's in pieces. Our perp is gone. He's not dumb.

In a loaned auto while at the stop light he lowered his window. The woman who had trapped on the windshield showed him the note written by his departed son's mother. He unlocked the passenger door and the woman got in.

She said to tell you one word. Enjoy. Then the oralling began with a red sheet covering her from head too the bottom of her flats.

The two left the city.

No one knew it but a stretch limo left the Nevada dessert and drove on into New Mexico. The driver drove into the dessert with a half full bottle of rose eighteen proof wine a black woman on his neck; fingers at the end of the ride his full blooded Lakota pecker.

Done was the first part of his revenge wrought for his dismembered son.

The second part done. He drove out of the dessert alone. The escaped criminals son's mom left behind, gutted.

Now to find the two god fathers and the father who shot his ex in her eye.

The news report came over the radio. There are still no leads to who was behind the president's assassination. China, Russia, Columbia zimbabwa and Afghanistan have all made speeches that the people are now better off. They have all refused to send any condolences.

This is Hal Crossfire and I say let this station take on all bets and cover any amount that this government is going to cover it up. And we all know why.

Again this is Hal Crossfire and that's the news for tonight. Tune in when we come back at nine p.m. good night.

Two months later the boarders on the north and coast lines were now not as severely guarded. The president's assassin had not be apprehended. This assassin would never be solved in the eyes of the public. This time unlike Kennedy's all of culprits would remain uncaught and unpunished.

There was some scattered chatter that loosening the boarder lines strangle hold would free a way to allow the assassin to escape. The people in the know had anticipated it and knew it would amount to zilch.

A phone call did come into the US Mexico border portal headquarters in Washington DC that twenty year old ice cream truck should only be a would be boarding crossing.

The call came from Washington DC itself, so there was little attention being paid to it, but the law stated should a boarded crossing lead come in pass it on directly. The call proved fruitful. In the ice cream truck's freezer were Glasni's remains.

The escaped prisoner was dismembering, eyes gouged out and tongue shoved up the crispy blackened corpses an spore.

Needless to say the truck leaving Mexico was convecated.

When the news casted the fate of former escape, the call came into Washington, DC's boarder Patrol Headquarters that the driver was paid to transport the truck and body with his full knowledge he was transporting a dead escaped American prisoner and that he knew the patrol would be tripped off. Further a taped audio recording was sent to the largest Washington news paper. The Mexican was set free only after a month long investigation, including personal visits to his family and neighbors in Juan Chupa, his home communities suburb. He was clean and his bank account had only a five hundred dollar deposit two weeks before his trek into the US prison system. One day later Joseph O'brian Pesci walked into his apartment. Pushing the first button to shout off his alarm he took full awareness the unarmed white light bulb was already on. Two seconds later he alerted his body be aware. A millisecond later his eyes closed.

No Excedrin awaited him upon his consciousness arousal. What did await him brought fear to accompany the aching earing, head bell clanging pain that came from the Johnson bar's crash against his cracked skull.

He was on his knees and forearms tied tightly and his chest and stomach uncomfortable over a metal beer keg.

A voice came. Do not talk until I finish asking you, so you know exactly what I want and how your answer determines how this little scene will play out.

Family maybe special to you, but choices sometimes need to be made. Here is a choice you will make in ten seconds. Your brother's where abouts or yours and you kids in your graves within three days. I will leave your if you choose the wrong answer wife alive to fuck her brains out after you and her kids are dead.

Before leaving Sheryl Lym Bey was allowed to leave the bed room. He had backoned her and Alonzo her four year old son.

Fear was in his eyes as the two stood before his eyes. She showed him a hand mirror and he realized he was naked. In her had was a small steal bladed hachet.

She and Alonzo walked behind him Tape was then put over his mouth while the little boy instructed by his mother took six swings and chopped of his privates. A child is involved here, so privates are written of in the stead of –c- and --- i-.

The two went on and the hatchet left with his assailent chopped off his head.

Riversend made sure no fingerprints were left opened, left, closed the door and headed for Blend, Montana.

CHAPTER NINETEEN

What do you need us to do? Nothing. The line went silent. At least he's still alive. Now put him out of your mind until he's finished. You are alert right now. But only in the event he goes too far. You got it?

If you ring me, um not to hesitate.

Right. So far he's just off the grid. We know why, so we're not pushing at him. At not now. That's it. See you later. You too.

Tiger Li Jung had been given their orders.

Skip. We're not going to get any new missions until he's back in the fold? Most likely, but as I'll do, stay sharp, skip line went dead, the rest pusher their end call button.

CHAPTER TWENTY

inez Bevery was having a little world with him. She had finally caught up to him in front of Manns, restaurant. The porkish looking Japanese female he arrived there with did of an arrogant bitchlike stare towards her, but the interruption was done with dignity and an utmost polite posture. She still struck a leer towards the intruder.

I know of someone in need of your special skills continued Einez. Please allow only a few minutes of your precious attentiveness.

Ling, please go to the table. I promise I will be in shortly. Ling Mu Ling conceded and the greeter gave her the table exactly as she ordered.

The conversation ended, and they're holding her fourteen year old until she makes them money enough to let her have her freedom. Those crackheads are never going to hold onto what they force her to make. You can win a large wages her child will be doing the same things they have her mother doing.

Names and some suspected addresses were given to him. Departure led her again to the federal Bureau of Investigation and he to Ling Mu Ling.

Found but a setting displeasing to launch his revenge. So close, so close, so close.

She still had a bit of eel morsel between her grinders. On the way to the taxi barn she kept tasting it. She had that opportunity to such it out or crab a minty toothpick. She chose the flavor.

The taxi driver never got out to let them in. He opened the door for her entry. Her panties exposed while her legs parted as she entered. The shock took hold of her immediately. She froze while her legs were still apart. The driver got a good long gander of a thing thong exposing a left vaginal lip.

He was a bit startled she left her legs open to that exposure. Further when he took a look why she was not being corrected. The body of her date started sliding to the sidewall. The whole was almost four inched across his forehead. Death so quick his face was not even showing a surprised. No statement except from the driver as the corpse hit the ground.

This one he did not care to hide. The news should have his last quarry aware he was the last of the three removing all the doubt why Glasni was found in pieces.

What he did not know is he was already being hunted. Usual in a hunt there is a prey. Not this time.

He was not sure but just in case, he kept his eyes wide open. He knew only a dunce could not realize his end pointed towards nearness. He knew where to wait. He chose a fling. He kept his head on two methods of death. Poison and explosives.

The first class flight still would not expose him. He had to expose himself.

It was long ago. The insurance company paid the full life insurance policy. Three quarters of a million dollars.

Already upper middle class she never changed her address. She had become easy to find.

The woman, a stranger to her followed her during the day. With the quietness of a butterfly the woman slept in her home while she slept without her knowledge.

When she went out Clichet, his allonym and Broken Arrow, his allonym stayed in her home without her knowledge.

Ben Neck, his allonym kept watch in shifts with Allnym, his allonym aw snipers. Even their own squad members could not see them. They were that good.

When this third godfather was to make a play it would not play.

His plain lander. He went directly to his son's mother's job at lunch.

She was surprised he had come. She had not known he was there even though she knew when he got the news of his son he would be there.

So dropped any breath she might have breathed until her tongue left his mouth. He knew what was next. He still bothered not to stop her slap.

The third godfather stood up and walked directly to them. You came here to kill me too. I know you knew I would come. Before it starts I think you should know. Your boy should have been treated worse that what we gave him.

Your boy raped these one hundred one children. He sodomized them all. Male and female. Here are their mothers in some cases addresses their names and ages, from three years old to twelve years old. In a couple cases their mothers and fathers lived together. Same age group. That is what it has all been about. You murdered two heroes you dumb fuck I wanted you to see my face when I told you. I will be here in case you still want to finish your illness. Your revenge.

Then seven men stood up in the lunchroom and walked to godfather number three, stood beside and the eight started to depart together.

Public or no public the Lakotan's squad members, Tiger Li Jung, stopped it all as they entered together. The war ended when he called them. It's over he said.

No more has been heard since. Two days later three South American drug lords surrounded by hundreds of armed soldiers, in three different camps committed suicide by hanging.

A day later Tiger Li Jung was back in Washington, DC Celebrating

THE END

Printed in the United States
by Baker & Taylor Publisher Services